COLOR ME BLUE

By Daniel Stone

For information contact; danielschlueteroffical@gmail.com
Book and Cover design by Daniel Schlueter
ISBN: 9781717858719
First Edition: October 2018
10 9 8 7 6 5 4 3 2 1

Other Works by Daniel Stone

The Mataline Prescon Series

Stars

Disclaimer:

This book contains mature themes. It is not suitable for children or anyone sensitive to themes of sexual assault.

Dedicated to those dyed the bleeding color blue.

Table of Contents

Part One

Blue

" Blue." I looked across the aisle. " Blue." It was my father. " Come here, child." He was standing, hands laced behind his back, head not turned to me. I stood slowly, the long fabric of my blue dress falling to the earth. I crossed the soft carpet and stood beside him. Beneath us, through the long, clean glass panes, a world of rolling hills moved. The hills were of dirty yellows and browns. " Why have you called me over?" I inquired, looking to my father's face. His blue skin was bunched around his forehead, as if he was thinking hard about something. His blue eyes stared down at the land under us, never once leaving. " To show you, to really show you, this." I looked at him and one of my blue eyebrows perked up, then I turned my gaze out the window of the Skytrain. My eyes found sprinkles of brown buildings and clusters of trees.

" Do you know why we ride this train, child?"

" No, father." I answered obediently. " We ride it because we are too important to scurry over the earth." I looked to him again, as confused as earlier. " That land down there, those. . .colors, if you want to call them that, are unfit to hold us." I looked back out the window and tried to make sense of my father's words.

" You're special, my child." I looked to him, this time he looked at me as well. " I never want you to lose sight of that, you're Blue; you are. . .me and you; so vital to this world."

" Because I am vital, I do not have to walk on the ground?" I asked, eyes wide. My father smiled gently, " You don't 'have' to walk there. Not if you don't desire to do so." I blinked and looked back out at the land. " What's so foul about it?" I wondered aloud. " Compared to you, everything is foul." he responded. " Even Yellow and Red?" I asked. This made him pause, I looked to him, he appeared worried, he considered his response carefully. " I would not say that. . . but you are equally important to them and you should never let them walk over you."

" What about Purple, Green, and Orange?"

" Below you."

" What about the colors down there?" I pointed to the earth. " Don't make me laugh, child." he said with a smile, " They're dirt and twigs; you are the ocean." he looked right at me. " You tell me which is more important."

" The ocean." I answered obediently and felt myself giddily happy. It was nice to be given such praise. " Precisely." he responded and I laughed softly. He grinned and stuck out a blue fist. I connected my fist carefully with his and then we pulled apart quickly, both saying " The ocean!" We laughed.

" Excuse me, my Blue." A voice suddenly interrupted our merriment. Father and myself both turned to see Purple, bowing slightly. " The train is having a slight issue and I am not sure what to do about it." Purple looked ashamed, a light violet raising in his purple face. My father sighed heavily, " Purples," he said, " what are they useful for?" he winked and I giggled. Purple shifted unhappily as my father looked to him, " Alright, show me where that problem is." Father then walked past him, vanishing behind the curtain of the control room. Purple hesitated a moment longer, staring at me with a gaze of undeterminable emotions, then he exited after father.

Purple

I wonder if I did not know I was purple how I would feel about myself. See the first thing I learned about myself was my color. The first words ever spoken to me. " You are Purple." I can close my eyes and remember them clear as day. Blue, my father, said them to me.

" This instrument?" Blue asked me, turning his intense yet calm face. We stood in the Skytrain's control room. " Yes, my Blue." I quickly answered. It was the train's conductor light that had given me the trouble. Blue nodded, " The readings on our plasma are too high, and what do we do when that happens?" I blinked at him. " I am not sure, . . .my Blue." Blue rolled his eyes and reached down to take off the panel from underneath the instrument. He pulled off the panel and leaned in to screw off the small cap of the silver engine, we could hear the small clunking noises it produced better now that its panel was removed. He looked in, squatting on the tips of his toes and I kneeled down beside him. He 'tch'ed with his teeth, " Look in here, boy." I obeyed and peered in, my neck straining a bit as I leaned in. " See how the color is a purplish-white? Feel the heat?"

" Yes, my Blue." I replied as I stared down into it, the color shined in my eyes; it looked a similar shade to me but lighter and more faint than my own skin. It sparked brightly and I winced away from the heat; purple drops of sweat forming along my face.

" That means you've let the crystals get too hot and they're starting to burn up."

" Burn?" I asked and he nodded. I made a face of confusion, "
But plasma crystals never have to be replaced, they are immortal
in that sense." He smiled softly and replied, " I see that Purple
did teach you something." I smiled and felt warmly pleased. To
have Blue praise me. . .wow, heh.

" But if you don't give the plasma crystals the right amount of
coolant, their immense heat will begin to melt each other."

" Oh." I replied and he nodded, I looked down at the floor and
doubted whether or not I should say my thought. " But um. . ."
His gaze perked up, surprised, " I put coolant in at the beginning
of the ride." Blue shook his head no. " Purple, listen, it's enough
in between our estate and the beach and perhaps Yellow's and
ours, but between Red's and ours?! One cup at the beginning of
our trip is not nearly enough! Jeez! It's a miracle we've never
got stuck out here before."

" I am very sorry, my Blue." I answered, bowing my head. He
stood up. " It's ok, we are only what people teach us." he smiled
understandingly. I blinked widely and went to add more coolant
to our engine, I heard my father pad away without so much as a
goodbye. I screwed the lid off the liquid's container and poured

some into the measuring cup, the liquid was a rich blue. I stared at it, a feeling of disappointment in my gut. I leaned into the cabinet and stared down at the purple shimmering crystals. My guts hurt as I drowned them in royal blue.

Blue

I returned through the rich blue curtain separating the control room and the riding carriage. My eyes instantly spotted my daughter, Blue, who stared out the window romantically. I chuckled under my breath, amused, it seemed she did not soak in my speech very well. Blue seemed to find the beauty in everything, sometimes so much so I feared she lost sight of the beauty in herself. I wondered if I was the same way once, perhaps my mother had taught it out of me when I was young and I just couldn't remember now. Blue looked a little like my mother now that I thought about it, they had the same full hair, although mother always had kept hers pinned up and somewhat short while Blue wore it long and free. They both were calm colors, I always thought I was a bit more high-strung than them but I supposed at heart we were all the same. Same flesh, same bones, same color.

" Daydreaming?" I asked, wandering up to her. I leaned an arm against the glass and stared out. The sky was sparkling blue as it should be. She chuckled softly, " Daydreaming is for children."

she reminded and I laughed, " Then it suits you just fine." She gave a pouty fake frown before grinning. I stared out and watched the silver clouds, like plumes of iron. The glass was warm from the sun and my arm felt it through my buttoned jacket. It was quiet for a moment and then Blue said, " You look good today, father." I smiled calmly, " Thank you." Some silence. " I heard Yellow plans to be there." she commented, she still had the child-like urge to make conversation just to make it. It took maturity to respect all that silence had to offer. I kept my eyes on the drifting skies. " Do you think they will come?" I asked her, curious of what she thought.

" No." she answered, " You know sometimes they don't show." I looked to her. " Why do you think they won't?" I inquired. She looked sad as she replied, " I think Yellow doesn't like me." I knew she was talking about Yellow's child. I sighed deeply and grabbed her shoulder, "So what if he doesn't, you can't place your worth in other people." She shook her head as if I didn't understand. She turned away and returned to her satin, cushioned seat. She sighed, crossed her arms, and stared out the window. I looked back out mine, she was so overemotional.

Blue

Father didn't understand. Yellow was incredible, I WANTED him to like me. Sure, I was his equal and yes, I was the ocean but HE was the brilliant sun! There has never been anyone as perfect.

The skytrain arrived a little later than planned, much to father's annoyance. Our speed had been slowed because of the engine's malfunction. Father had called Purple in and lectured him harshly over it; he apparently had waited a bit to inform us. He had bowed and apologized profusely, looking quite embarrassed when looking to my father. Looking very strange when he looked to me.

" Lovely, lovely to see you again!" Yellow embraced my father at the bottom of the skytrain station, at the back of Red's Mansion. I looked up and the red fiery walls stretched all the way up into the gorgeous bluesky. I didn't like it. " Oh my gosh! You look greeeeaaatt!" I looked over and my father was chuckling, slightly abashed, and I grinned. Yellow was very nice. Her yellow skin was shown off on her bare arms and exposed shoulders and collarbone. She wore a large, puffy dress, so light and bright; like cotton and stars. Nothing like my plain blue satin.

" Blue! Blue! Blue!" She ran and embraced me, choking me in her bright, strong, so strong, grip. She was taller than me and her smile was wider than her face. She pulled away, still holding my shoulders. " Oh my gosh! You're so taaallllll, oh my! You look darling, darling!" I laughed lightly and blushed. " Thank you." I stated passively. She grabbed my hair and held it up. " Soooo lonnnnggg." I never understood Yellow, I liked her but I never understood her, perhaps I never will. " Shall we go inside?" my father asked to spare me. " Oh, yes-yes!" Yellow gushed, turning. " Red, Red, and my child are all here!" She made a dramatic pouty face. " I wanted Yellow to come greet you with me but he refused." She groaned, " Such an unsocial child." and began to stalk back towards the mansion.

I looked to my father, gaining my own pouting face, and whispered, " I told you he doesn't like me." He frowned and began to follow Yellow. He rolled his eyes, " Such an overemotional child." he complained aloud.

Later, I sat in the sitting room, banished to the kid table again. I looked over to the primary adults, laughing around the decadent red table. I looked around, red walls, red ceiling, red floor; colors, never realized how sick this place made me. I sighed.

" Hey!" Red complained across from me. He was short, only eight, and CONSTANTLY unhappy. He slammed his toy truck down grumpily. " Listen to me!"

" Sorry, sorry." I apologized, even though I wasn't sorry, " Go ahead." He frowned and pulled on his short flame hair " You stink, Blue! You gotta listen!!" I frowned, " I am. I am. Go ahead." He placed his cheek in his red hand, smushing it to his face. " I'm not so sure I want to marry you. You don't listen." I cocked my head curiously. " Marry?" I inquired. He retorted, " What about it?" curtly, looking back to his truck and rolling it back and forth along the red tablecloth. I blinked widely. " What is 'marry'?" I asked calmly, perhaps something he had made up? He chortled.

" It's not a thing like that, it's something you do." He said it as if it was the simplest thing in the world. " Well, what do you do?" I asked. He scowled, " If I told you," he replied tersely, " you wouldn't listen anyway."

" Yellow?" I inquired and Purple shook her head, "Sorry, my Blue, haven't seen him." I tried to not look crushingly disappointed. I saw other Purple, ours, ascending the staircase of. . .red. I jogged over and called, " Purple, have you seen

Yellow?" He paused, he had a stack of folded fabrics in his hands; red, fuzzy towels. " At the dining table with your father, my Blue." he answered calmly. I frowned, not that Yellow! Ugh, my father was right; Purples weren't good for anything. Want someone found, better find them yourself! I joined him on the staircase and beat up the red stairs and red comforting carpet. Call the interior decorator. He's fired.

" Never mind, I'll find him myself!" I announced and I didn't look back to see Purple's reaction.

Purple

" I'm so dumb!" I cursed aloud, holding a hand to my face in disappointment. Teacher laughed and took the towels from my hands. I had descended to the bottom of the staircase to gripe. " Common mistake, it's really ok." she assured, placing a hand to my shoulder. " But I should have known!" I carried on. " Why would child Blue be asking for adult Yellow?! So dumb. . ." She patted my shoulder awkwardly. " You'll get better, promise! They have an odd way of speaking that's all. I mean why don't they just call the children 'Jr.' or I don't know, maybe an actual name?!" She laughed as if sharing some private, inside joke. I frowned. " But don't we just call each other Purple, isn't everyone like that?"

She shook her head no. She praised, " Good try though."

I placed the towels on the red, shiny shelf, with seashell detailing in the master bathroom. Red's room, the grown one's that is. I looked at the rose ocean shells and smiled lightly, what was this? A sea of blood? I turned to exit the bathroom, it had his giant tub and three sinks. All red. All scarlet. Florid to the bone. I paced over the floor, red tile, making very little noise. Then, abruptly, I heard a slam from outside, and a harsh sound like something just hit something else. Wondering what the clatter was, I wandered casually to the door, open just a bit. The lights inside the bathroom were dim, I had only turned on one of what had to be elven bulbs. My eyes widened.

Red, senior, and Blue, my father, were near the door and something was off about their body language. My instincts instantly knew. Red had large arms on either side of Blue and Blue was staring him straight in the eye, but he was sweating. Rich, blue drops. " Been waiting to get my hands on you." Red said and the tone was husky and purr-like. A cat. Blue crossed his arms over his chest. " Don't see why you would." he replied stoically. " You're damn sexy, that's why!" Red retorted, his voice like bubbles bursting by needle. Blue winced at the curse, I leaned a little further forward. What was happening? " Red, please." Blue stated, as if speaking to a petulant child. He tried to step to the side but Red didn't budge, and Red's arm blocked Blue's escape.

" Please what?" Red asked tauntingly. Blue stiffened and tightened the cross of his arms over his chest. " Let me go." Blue stated firmly. Red moved his head forward into the crook of Blue's neck. Blue gasped and I heard a messy, almost slurping sound. Blue shoved him away and protested, " No!"

" No?" Red retorted, stabling himself after being shoved a step back, " No." Blue confirmed. Red smirked. " Oh well, aren't you a regular stand-up, Blue. You sit there all dinner teasing me with your body, like a little slut; you brushing my leg with those thick thighs. You're begging for it, always begging for it, and now you're trying to tell me no?" Blue's face grew flushed and he leaned back, as if to make more space between him and Red.

" None of that's true and I can say no if I want to."

" Oh," Red exclaimed, " always so entitled. Not everything is about what you want, Blue." He poked Blue's shoulder harshly. Blue looked indignant and moved his shoulder away from the finger. This was fucking weird. I stepped away from the door

and ran my fingers through the top part of my purple hair, that was tied tightly to my scalp, feeling stressed. Damn Primaries! What do I do? I've been in here too long to just leave now. Who knows what they'll do to me if they how much I've heard! Crap.
. .

" Red. . ." The voice was wary. " Blue. . ." The voice was full of lust. I heard a crash and cry and clatter and decided it was about time to get the fuck out of here. I ran over to window quietly. It was cloudy cause this was the bathroom. Privacy, ya know.

" Red, please stop!"

I quietly, but oh so quickly, threw open the latch and pushed the window up, the pane only somewhat heavy. The bathroom was filled with outdoor light as it was opened, so were my purple eyes. Ouch. I pushed myself up and sat upon the window frame. I stared out the side of the mansion. I had to be four stories up, the wall of fire going down, down. The ground looking so small. I gulped.

" Please s-stop!" I glanced one last time to the door and then slipped off the window, my purple fingers gripping on the frame like my life depended on it, because, well, it did.

Blue

The water was a calming warm. It splashed up around my chest as Red entered the tub before settling after he sat. He sighed happily, " Nothing like a good, passionate fuck before a bath, right, Blue?" I scowled and looked over to the red wallpapered wall. " Oh, come on," he complained light-heartedly, " you know you enjoy our little escapades." He poked me, in the stomach, with one of his toes. I begrudgingly glanced back at him and grumbled, " If you mean dread, then yes."

" Oh?" he responded, placing an exaggerated hand to his chest, " Dread? You flatter me." He grinned devilishly and leaned over the side of the tub, opening a red woven bag. I frowned, I didn't know how that could possibly be received as a sort of compliment. I gave up watching him and ran my hands down my blue legs. The water felt nice, in an empty kind of way.

" Want a glass?" he asked and I looked over to see him holding a tall champagne bottle and glass. " No, I don't exactly feel eager to receive anything from you."

" Not willingly anyway." he replied and chuckled at his joke. My guts burned with anger. He was so disgusting! Infuriating! I just didn't understand what could make anyone so volatile! So awful, so deplorable! I didn't respond, only glared, and he poured the red champagne into a clear glass. He offered it out to me and I crossed my arms in refusal. He shrugged carelessly and took a big sip himself. He placed the bottle back down on the floor.

" I really should get Purple to put a table in here, beside the tub." he commented, laying a bare red arm along the tub's back wall. He looked way too relaxed for what had just happened, but then again I suppose I was too calm as well. I looked up to the ceiling, red, and looked at the small amber bulbs. " Blue, whatcha thinkin' about?" Red bothered, couldn't he just leave me alone?

" Nothing." I stated firmly and he frowned. " That's a lie, you're such a liar."

" Better than a rapist." I retorted snappishly and he smiled, excited by the exchange.

" Oh! Oh wow," he leaned back so his red back touched the porcelain wall. " Did Blue just. . .speak up for himself?" he laughed, " A rapist?! Ha! You're too cute." He grinned wickedly, "It's not rape if you want it."

" But I didn't and don't want it!" I exclaimed, I remember being VERY clear about that. He was actually insane! He smirked, " I beg to differ."

" What do you mean 'beg to differ'?!" I was screaming now. " It's not up for debate!" I stood up, that's it; I was out of here! I should have left the moment the sick act was done! But I. . .I just felt so dirty, I thought maybe the water could wash it away. I should know by now that you never truly felt clean again. Red looked so horribly smug as I got out, he was staring everywhere he shouldn't have been. I hopped out and felt the chill of the outside, I glanced and realized the window was open. I wandered over and closed it, looking at the outside landscape of trees and mountains until they were blocked by the purposefully clouded window. I stared at the opaque glass and took a deep breath. Red suddenly commented, " Your ass is fucking A-mazing." I twitched irritably and snatched a soft red towel on the shelf to my right. I quickly wrapped it around my waist and glared down at my bare, moist feet, on the red tile like a bed of hot coals.

" I love this." he said and I heard the water shift, as if he had laid back, " Like two lovers bathing together after sex." He sipped his champagne. Like was the key word.

Blue

This door had to be the one! I had checked nearly the entire second floor of the Red Mansion for Yellow, he was as elusive as a blue bird. I watched the sky from my bedroom as a child, fascinated by the way their wings stretched above their heads and pushed them through the sky. There were a lot of black and brown birds. Some had small patches of red or orange, but there was so few blue ones. I noticed that.

Barren. This room was unused it seemed. I stepped in and wondered why that was. In every other room I had been in, even if it had no functional purpose, the room was ornate. Always ready for guests. Startling, obnoxious, red vases and portraits, chandeliers, and loveseats. This room was dusty it seemed. It was red, cause nothing in this house could escape the color, but it lacked most of the trademarks of the Red Mansion, like a fancy rug or, I don't know, lighting. There was a long bookshelf of brown next to the tall window. Light streamed in, making a rectangle of luminescence on the empty floor. I walked in and looked around. I blinked at the bookshelf, it seemed unreal, maybe holy even. The one non-red thing in this entire house.

I traveled more slowly after that and took my time wandering into and carefully observing each room I checked. As if there was something precious there, something I had been blind to before. When I exited a larger, decadent room with a red piano, don't ask me how they got it that color, I was met in the hallway by Green. She had eyes that were wide and hair that was long, her green attire was a long loose dress stopping at her ankles. She wore no shoes.

" My Blue," she dipped into a bow, " how wonderful to see you." I asked, " Have you seen Yellow, younger." I added as an afterthought, beginning to lose my faith in Secondary colors. " Of course," Green grinned, " why would it be the Elder? That makes no sense." She was preaching to the choir. " He is upstairs, the third floor, five sitting rooms in, counting from the left staircase." I smiled widely, " Thank you!" I exclaimed and then sprinted to the left staircase. I exactly knew his location; I had been coming here since my childhood after all.

The steps were plentiful yet their climb did not slow my eager speed. Yellow had finally been found thanks to Green and I was going to get to him before he could go slip away to some other hiding spot.

This room was unlike the others, more muted in its decadence. There was a round table of rich wood in the middle of the room, holding a red globe and florid candle holders and their occupants, unlit as for now. I'm sure if they were lit, they'd burn red fire, don't look at me like that, they'd find a way. He sat by the long, tall, rectangular window of the room, signature to the Red Mansion. His chair was plush and, what else, red. His yellow skin and suit stood out against it like a drop of mustard at a murder scene. I wandered over and sat in a matching seat on the other side of the window, across from him. I smiled awkwardly, teeth almost grit. He looked to me calmly and then, wordlessly, turned his head back to the window. Told you he was less than fond of me. I felt a drop of sweat find me and I shifted unnaturally to gaze through the glass too.

Mountains in the distance, the Flame Peaks, as prominent in our eyes as they appeared on the globe, back beyond us on the table. The sky was a light blue, with peppering, fickle clouds.

" Blue." he stated and I smiled, immediately turning my whole attention and body to him. He was glaring at me hard. " You're desperate and it's honestly trying, try and tone it down."

" . . ." He looked back out the window and my smile was uncomfortably held on my face. Wasn't he a true romantic? Oh gosh.

Purple

I decided I hated my life in that moment and I hated father too. And Red and especially her, ya know what? They were worthy of my hate, I was tired of suppressing it. Although I suppose the word 'tired' should not be uttered, considering my location. My arms ached and hands hurt from gripping into the rock. There were few handholds and I might have been dehydrated with all the sweat dripping off me and falling three plus stories to the ground where they went- splat.

My lungs were choked with tension and I was shaking slightly. Maybe it wasn't such a good idea to start hating the most powerful beings I knew right now. Maybe I should start begging forgiveness instead and hope for some kind of Primary intervention. My leg dubiously lowered down and touched around for a crook. The wind blew against me strongly, as I clung to the exterior of the Red Mansion, and I gave a quiet noise of distress. If this was the best plan I could come up with to get out of that situation, I was utterly stupid and needed to return to my apprenticeship; probably needed to do that anyway. This was terrifyingly stupid. I found a hold or two in the rock and lowered myself. Finally, there was another window, I looked down and could see it, thank Primaries! I was gonna enter it even if it was Yellow's bathroom and she was showering! I was gonna die out here! The fall to the ledge was a little farther than I would have liked and my feet dangled in the air momentarily. I quickly lowered myself, my arms as aflame as these fucking walls, and my feet touched the bottom of the window's ledge. My arms quickly grasped the top of the pane and I smirked in relief and looked in. Blue, young, and Yellow, same, were both sitting there. Blue was utterly shocked and Yellow, mildly curious. Oh come on. Well maybe one more window, I decided, but before I could climb away, Blue opened the window, shoving the glass upward after unlatching the lock. She grabbed me by the waist and I was extremely uncomfortable, for seemingly EVERY reason to ever be conceived. She dropped me on the ground and Yellow stood to look down at me, maybe a bit suspiciously.

" Purple?!" Blue exclaimed, probably the first time I've heard her raise her voice today, between her and father that made two shrieking Blues. " What were you doing out there?! Do you have any idea how dangerous that is?!" No, I only imagined my body breaking and twisting in ways it never had before for fun.

" Yes, my Blue." I answered and wondered if I should stand back up, I was on my knees where she dropped me, or if that would seem impudent. " You could have fallen, Purple! What were you thinking?!" she barked wildly. I didn't know why she sounded so distressed, although there was more anger than concern there I think. " Do you know how upset my father would be if you died?!" Somewhat inconvenienced, I mentally replied, I wasn't exactly the apple of father's eye. Blue looked vexed, perplexed, and crossed her arms over her chest.

" I am sorry, my Blue." I bowed my head and wished she would stop lecturing me. I knew it was dangerous! I wasn't THAT braindead! Made my blood boil! She was the ignorant one! She didn't know the situation!

" Why were you climbing outside?! That is unacceptable! I demand an explanation!"

" You were trying to jump?" Yellow asked and I stared over to him with a disbelieving glance. " Jump?!" Blue exclaimed in horror, considering Yellow's suggestion as a probable theory. Honestly that, might be easier to explain. " No, my Yellow." I answered and Blue exhaled strongly, " Well, that's good." she said with a relieved smile. " Yes, my Blue." I replied awkwardly, not knowing exactly what to say.

" So then, why were you?!" she further pressed with an angry look. Why do you even care?! I internally raged, I'm just an incompetent Purple! Why do you care what happens to me?! I'm so slow I can't even keep up with your nonsensical, identical names! . . . I can't keep up with their names. . . " I saw a stone fallen from its place on the Mansion's wall. I thought it was a shame and I wanted to fix it." I looked off to the side, giving a shameful, pitiful expression, " I'm so sorry I've upset you." There was silence as Blue and Yellow soaked in the lie.

" A stone?!" Blue yelled and I winced, looking back over to them. Yellow had his face in his hand, looking incredibly disappointed, almost disbelieving. " What are you?! A stone mason?!" she proclaimed, " Purple, the stone mason?!" I felt real shame now. She didn't have to be so lacking in understanding. Sure, it was a foolish fake decision but fake me had done it for the sake of the Primaries. Couldn't she be a little kinder?

She smacked me on the head, not too harshly, but enough for me to be surprised. " Idiot! That's dangerous. Next time, just report it to someone who actually knows what they're doing." She huffed and turned to Yellow, " Purples! What are they good for?" He looked me straight in the eyes and grinned, " Nothing." he said.

I stood up quickly and felt miserable. Like shit! Like nothing. I was so angry and frustrated, why were they like this?! Entitled brats younger than me, scolding me?! She smacked me! Like a disobedient house dog! I turned to leave and hoped vengefully Red fucked her father good. So good, she felt it in her fucking cunt!

" Purple," Blue stated, " I didn't give you permission to leave." She was calm now. I stopped. Took another step forward. Stopped. Couldn't disappoint teacher. Didn't wanna know what would happen. Spun around, " Sorry, my Blue. I just want to inform someone who is smart about this stuff about the stone, so they can fix it." I smiled as if there was nothing but stuffing in my head. She paused a moment and then smiled, " Ok, go on then." She said it as if I was a child who really wanted a sweet. " Yes, thank you, Blue." I regretted the lie. Shoulda looked her in the face. Shoulda told her the truth. Shoulda watched her WEEP.

Blue

I had come downstairs and was looking for my child. Red ran up to me, " Blue!" he whined with his high voice, and pulled on the bottom of my jacket passionately, " Blue left me alone!" he complained. I smiled and snatched the child in his cute red suit up by the waist. He gave a squeal of delight, " Well, we can't have that!" I announced and pronounced, " We'll have to find her!"

" Yay!" Red exclaimed. I put him on my shoulders and he grabbed my head to stabilize himself. It hurt only a little bit, I missed the time Blue was a child, one in size, not spirit; she still was one of those now. She pretended to not like such games, any tickling, or rough-housing, but she did. And because she could deny she liked them, she liked them even more.

" Blue!" Red called out and it was pretty obvious who he was referring to. " Blue!" I began to walk through the the hallways, that girl had probably ran off to find Yellow, sometimes she made little sense. Thought he didn't like her and yet sought after him insistently. If I suspected someone didn't like me, I steered clear of them. Red sighed and relaxed his frame. " She doesn't listen, ya know?" he groused quietly.

" Blue?" I questioned and I imagined he nodded as he let out a 'hm' of confirmation. " How am I supposed to marry someone who doesn't listen?" he asked and I paused before laughing brightly.

" Marry?! By gosh, why would you ever want to do that?! One of those queer peasant traditions?" I shook my head and smiled, what a ridiculous, childish idea. " Because I don't want to be lonely." Red answered defensively and he ran his fingers through my shoulder length hair.

" Lonely? Why you'll be with your father and eventually your child, and you'll always have a Purple around, not to mention your Orange." He blew out air between his teeth.

" Daddy says I'm not supposed to fraternize with the help. He says I should keep my eyes on the prize."

I cocked up an eyebrow, still feeling humor, " What prize?"

" Blue." he replied. I paused my eager stride and felt something like dread in my chest. " Blue?" I questioned and Red chirped, " Uh-huh!" from above my head, " But she doesn't listen so I'm not sure why I SHOULD marry her."

" Does your father think you should marry Blue?" I asked and dubiously began to walk forward again. Was Red plotting something I didn't know about? Red seemed to think this over. " I don't know." he said finally and I asked, " What was his reaction when you told him about marrying her?" Red got quiet again.

" He, um, laughed." I felt an exhale leave me. Thank goodness, Red thought it was ridiculous as I did. No plots afoot. " Then he got quiet and scary." I was confused, " Scary?" Red made a short, subdued hum.

" When Daddy goes into the kitchen and starts drinking and screaming. That's scary." What? " Do you ever do that, Blue? Drinking and screaming?" he asked neutrally. I looked off into the red carpet I had been traveling over. Like a burning, scorching field.

Only sometimes.

" No, of course, I don't. That's not the best way to deal with your emotions." I stated with calm assurance, careful not to condemn Red with my words. No child should think negatively of their parent. Red gave another soft noise, " Works for daddy." he replied callously.

" Well, I'm sure he could do something else." I said unsurely and quickly added, " But that shouldn't have to be your concern, just stay away from your daddy when he's like that, ok?" Red exclaimed, " Well, duh." condescendingly, " Do you want me to get my head bashed in?" He exploded into loud laughter and kicked his legs lightly, them hitting my shoulders. I tightened my grip on his legs so he didn't fall.

We found them on the third floor, laughing like maniacs at something they couldn't stop laughing long enough to explain.

Blue

" A stone mason?! Purple, a stone mason?" Yellow was bent over, tears in his eyes. My gut hurt so bad but I couldn't stop. He thought I was funny! He was laughing with me!

" How dumb do you have to be?!" I exclaimed in between laughter and Yellow collapsed back into his chair. " Next time I get a mark on my floor, I'll call Purple! Since he's-he's a construction color now!" He slapped his knee and by gosh was it funny! By gosh, wasn't he gorgeous?! All happy like that! My father stood in the doorway and Red was sitting on his shoulders, heatedly lecturing me, but I didn't care, I was funny!

And Yellow was happy! We were so happy!

Finally we stopped and I had this smug, confidence that touched me all over. I spun the globe aimlessly as Father said some gentle things about us including Red in our fun and games. I just kept passing glances over to Yellow, who returned them. We were delinquent teenagers our parents couldn't hope to understand. Our secret, one idiot Purple and a window. I hoped years later we'd be able to call back on this moment with much fondness, I hoped Yellow remembered it as the moment he began to see me as more than just an annoyance. I hoped he would recall this moment as the time he began to love me as I loved him. . .

I had begged my father to let us stay the night, Yellow always stayed the night. . .but he had refused! He always did, he was such a stick in the mud. We formally said goodbye to the four of them and I hope Yellow did not forget our special joke. I widely smiled and spoke calmly, as I had known to do around the other Primaries since I could walk. It wasn't till we wandered out to the station did I give Father a true ear-full.

" Father! How am I supposed to bond with Yellow if you are always tearing me away from him?!" He rolled his eyes, he never took me seriously. " Yellow gets to stay the night. Why can I not?!"

He scowled and looked to me, " Maybe because you are thinking with your genitals instead of your head?" I gasped. " How dare you make that accusation!" I exclaimed and he brought a hand to to hold his temple. " I just want to TALK to him!" We entered the skytrain's door Purple held open.

" Blue, that is quite enough." he stated as he entered in and took a seat in our plush, blue seats. " You will stop your screaming." He narrowed his blue eyes and I huffed and sat back in my seat. Father sucked! He didn't get it! Yellow actually sounded like he liked me today! If I didn't keep the ball rolling, his affection might die and I'd be back at square one. He stared at the book, he pulled off the seat next to him. Its title: 'Mountains and How to Navigate Them.' I frowned. He had been reading that on the way here too.

" Have you ever even been on a Mountain?" I asked bitterly and Father looked over the top of his book. " Course not. Why would a Primary ever go somewhere dangerous?"

I paused, " Are mountains dangerous?" He shrugged and glanced back down at the page, " Apparently." I clicked my tongue in between my teeth.

" I bet Yellow would let her child go to a mountain." I muttered, sitting back in my seat; crossing my arms indignantly.

Father retorted, emotionlessly, still staring at his page, " This isn't about Mountains, this is about you wanting to have intercourse with Yellow." I blushed and frowned and Purple froze, mid-step, to look at us with a half shocked-half disgusted expression. " I-I don't want to have intercourse with him!" I protested and Father turned the page, " You can lie all you want, it won't change the truth."

" I don't! For real!" I barked and he said, " Ok, liar." I gave a sound of exasperation. Father was the absolute worst. Purple awkwardly shuffled into the control room and I thought it was a blessing. The less time I had to spend confined in here with my father, the better!

The trip started off slowly, the car raising into the air as it always did. I watched out the window, because it was that or stare at Father, I had brought no book. The trees were like pinpricks we had gotten so far up. I was used to the skytrain, I had been riding in it since I was a child. It was as home as Father's piano room or my bedroom, so I was very surprised when the entire thing rocked. We had been in the air a full ten minutes.

I looked to Father, very surprised and confused, and I could see he was scared. His eyes were as wide as china plates. As endless as the sky he fell out of. He jumped up and entered the control room briskly. I stood up, " Father?" The train rocked again, hard, and I fell. The carpet was soft under my hands. I heard snapping and cracking. It rocked again. I was on my hands and knees. " F-father?" Something was wrong with the train. In my gut, I knew it was bad. " Father!" A snap; horrible, loud, and final. I screamed as I flew up and smashed into the ceiling. I cried out, my head hitting the metal sharply. We were falling or, I was flying. I couldn't move, not even my eyelids, my eyes remaining open and there was this opposing wind causing tears to appear in them. What-there was this sensation of free-falling. Why-I couldn't move. How-father. A crunch. Snapping, screaming, metal eating itself. Something flying, my lungs tied, throat speechless. Eyes full of tears. I was thrown to the floor and the carpet was no longer soft. My knee crackled with agony. Everything was suddenly gone. Deep, dark, black.

Purple

When I woke up, there was this clear, light purple smoke everywhere. I coughed, my lungs rejected it. I glanced back and my legs were trapped by a large metal piece of the skytrain. I looked around and my heart began to pound. Purple sweat filling every pore. Through the smoke, I could see these tall shadows of what could have been horrid monsters looming over me. I cried and dug my fingers into the ground. My fingers pierced it. I looked down and my fingers were gone. The earth ate them.

Blue

A cry. I blinked and my vision was crushed petals. I blinked and blinked and everything hurt. My eyes started seeing shapes or maybe they were making them. I had something over me. I looked. Crumpled metal. I blinked. How? Where was I? Under me was, metal? Should be carpet, right? I was in the skytrain, right? I shook my head. No! This was wrong! Where were the chairs? Where was Father? Purple? Where was 'Mountains and How to Navigate Them?'

Purple

Dirt. The ground was dirt. My fingers were still there. I cried again and tried to pull myself forward. Pain. My legs were stuck.

" Help please!" I called into the smoke, " Someone, help me! My Blue, my Blue, where are you?!"

Blue

My Blue, my Blue? That was me. Was that Purple? Where was that idiot? He should be driving this thing. I smiled and tears found my eyes again. Had that incompetent fool somehow crashed us? If anyone could accomplish crashing a train that went along pre-set cables, it was Purple. Cables, snapping. I grit my teeth and fisted my hands. It made sense.

Purple

The smoke billowed upward. No one was answering. I looked to the dirt and I wondered if they were dead. The skytrain has crashed. We had been hit? Why? By what? When Blue came through the curtain, I thought maybe I had forgot to put the cooling solute in the engine again, but. . .I was wrong. I could see it in his eyes. I could see it was over.

Blue

The voice, which I thought was Purple, quieted. I tried to get to my hands and knees but my back met the metal and I screamed. It punctured my blue skin.

Purple

A scream. I was not alone. High-pitched. Blue? " Blue!" I cried, " Blue, are you alive?!"

Blue

Loaded question. I bit my teeth as tears dropped to the fucking metal ground. How did this happen?! I dropped down and felt the metal slide out of my flesh. I wailed, it sounded disgusting.

Purple

" Blue!" " Blue!" " Blue!" She was here! I wasn't alone! Purple tears dropped down my face, " Blue! Can you move?! I need you! Blue, can you hear me?!"

Blue

He was calling for me, and to him I would go. I began to slowly army crawl forward so I wouldn't brush the dangerous ceiling. The light came in at the end of the smashed carriage. I pulled my body out and fell to the ground. Smoke.

Purple

I heard no more cries and for a moment my hope fell and I feared I was alone. Feared those were her last cries. . .but then I heard something hit the ground.

Blue

The ground was soft, the smoke stung my eyes; I coughed. I shoved my hands into the unfamiliar earth and forced my body to stand. Everything hurt. My back was slick from what I knew was my own blood. My left leg could barely hold weight. " Purple!" I shouted, and I coughed again, " Call out to me! Purple!"

Purple

I cried, she was alive. She was speaking, she was coming to get me. " My Blue, I am trapped! My legs, follow my voice, please!"

Blue

I limped forward as I listened, with strong will, for his voice. It was hard because my ears were ringing. My vision, or the smoke, spun like a top. One foot in front of the other. I waved the smoke away, and I nearly stepped on his hand.

Purple

Her soft-shoed foot was right beside my hand. " My Blue!" I called out joyously.

Blue

I kneeled down and grabbed his face with my hands. I dug my nails into his cheeks, he cried out abruptly, expression changing from relief to fear. His eyes grew as I grit out, " What did you do?" His eyes were large and scared. " Nothing, my Blue."

" Bullshit!" I slammed his head into the ground. " What did you do?! You MORON!"

Purple

My head hit the earth harshly. This was the end. How horribly ironic, the Primary I thought was coming to save me was going to kill me. How fitting, how fitting to be killed by a girl of the same blood, by the same father; the one I always looked to and thought, why not me? The one I always wanted to be.

Blue

I slammed his head down again, " Why did you do it, Purple? As vengeance?! As retribution?! As an ACCIDENT?!"

Purple

I didn't do it. But then again maybe I did. How could she have known?

Blue

A scream like terror and death escaped my throat. I shoved his head down hard one last time and then stood up. " I demand an explanation." I stated harshly, " Later." I called and turned my body, " Father! Father?!"

Purple

I hoped she left me to die. I didn't want to be alive anymore.

Blue

He wasn't responding. Dread filled my chest. " Father?!" My heart began pound like a rabbit on caffeine. " Father?!" I began to wander across the clearing, " Father!" I would call for him until he responded to me. He HAD to respond to me. He just HAD to. The smoke was slowly starting to clear. I could see heaps of metal everywhere, twisted, gnarled, it had lost a fight with gravity and the ground. Glass was shattered and everywhere, under my feet like an ocean of brokenness. " Father?!"

" Blue. . ." The voice was faint. I screamed, " Where are you?!" I needed him NOW. " Blue. . ." I tried to make my ears track the noise. I wished they were stronger so they could locate Father exactly, like a hound catches the caffeinated rabbit. I walked towards the voice, hesitantly, not trusting the direction my feet had picked.

" Blue. . ." I spotted him. He was lying under a blue torn curtain, that once separated the carriage and control room. I quickly came to his side and his hair was wet with blood. His smile was weak but there. " Blue. . ." I gripped one of his hands, which had a shard of a glass sticking out of it. " Father. . ." My eyes were welling up again. His face was cut and his beautiful blue eyes were vacant. " Father! Stay with me!" I brought his head onto my knees and brought my head down to his chest so I could weep close to him. " Please, by goodness! I NEED you!" He gave a soft chuckle. " I thought all you needed was Yellow and a romance novel." I cried harsher, now was not the time for joking. I pulled up and said, " 1 love you! I love you!" Because I felt it was time for important things. The smile grew wider on his face. " Oh, Blue, I did nothing to deserve a girl as good as you." His eyes glowed with a dim love. His hand lightly gripped mine. " I love you too. So much. . ." My face was so wet. Why was this happening?

" You'll be ok, right?!" I exclaimed. I couldn't deal with goodbye. He blinked and it took him such a long time to open his eyes again. " We all die, Blue." My tears were so big. He looked past me to the sky. " I just didn't think I would go so early. . ." His smile grew a bit, " I, at least, wanted to see the see the aftermath of you and Yellow's first hookup, that would have been great fun." I looked down at his bleeding chest, his jacket was soaked. He had lost so much. " Please don't joke." I begged, " Not about this, I don't want you to leave. . ." A sob choked me. He tenderly smiled, " I don't want to either, the world is beautiful, Blue, and so are you, I wanted to live in it with you." He coughed up some blue. I was horrified. " I wanted-"

" Save your strength!" I pleaded, " You can make it! It doesn't have to be the end! We can live together, Father! I NEED you!"

He rubbed my hand with his own, they were moist from sweat and blood. " I love you, I'm sorry I have to go."

" No, Father, please!"

" Don't trust Red, I don't know but I suspect he's plotting something." I paused my screaming, I would listen to my father's words, hang on to them, " Don't obsess over this, move on; you will be happier. Don't turn people away, accept help." My grip tightened. " Don't give up hope. Stand up for yourself. You're the best thing I've ever made. You're my ocean." He smiled warmly and he was crying too. " I love yo. . ."

. . .No. . .no. . . My tears were endless, my weeping a waterfall; sobs a rainstorm. The only thing in my ocean was sorrow. A miserable ocean of death and tears fit only for a wretched, fatherless girl.

I lifted the broken piece of metal off of Purple's legs. It was heavy but my arms felt no strain of its weight. I was convinced I would not feel anything anymore. Numb, stunned, static. At least then nothing would have to change, I would never have to deal with what had happened. Still couldn't-why couldn't-I didn't-he wouldn't-. Purple pulled his legs out and I dropped the piece down, it landing with a heavy thump in the earth. " Thank you, my Blue." he said and bowed his head, pulling his legs close to himself. He was right to be respectful and cautious. I felt like if he misstepped I'd kill him right now. Like I was walking on eggshells and one Purple word out of turn and they'd all crack, like his skull would. Like I would.

" Can you stand?" I questioned, not an ounce of concern in my voice. He looked up and purple blood stained his face in disheartened lines. " I think so, my Blue." He began to stand up and swayed slightly, his legs shaking. He looked to me once fully erect. His hair was everywhere, slightly singed in places, all torn from his neat back ponytail, as tiny as it was. I frowned, " Do you think you can carry a body?"

" A body?" he returned and my gaze tightened like a coiling whip. He was filled with realization. " Blue's dead." The words hung and I wished he had never uttered them. " No." I stated firmly, he looked to me in surprise, " I'm right here." It was final. He nodded slowly.

" Yes, my Blue." he replied and then we fell to silence. " . . .What now?" he asked after a moment. I glared at him and then pointed off in the direction we had come from. He turned his whole head to follow it. " We go back to Red's Mansion, you explain yourself, and I stress about whether to kill you or not." He swallowed dryly. He was too weak to carry Father and I didn't want to. If the flesh turned cold in my Blue hands, there would be no escape.

I turned and began to walk. There was this stretching moment in which I heard no footsteps behind me. Then they occurred, quiet, dubious, just as everything I heard, as if the whole earth had fallen silent for a single funeral.

Purple

Still wanted to die a little bit. She just made me confront how absolutely useless and expendable I was. Her father had just died, didn't have the heart to say our anymore, I-I couldn't believe it. My legs hurt and I could tell one had a large, deep gash in the area around my calf but I didn't want to stop and check it. She said she was thinking about killing me. . .maybe I should have been more scared, but honestly I felt as dead as Blue back there.

" Why did you do it?" she asked, not stopping to glance at me. " The skytrain?" I replied and her fists tightened by her sides. " Of course, what else would I be speaking of-" Her voice was taunt, if a voice could be such a thing. I should have carefully crafted a plead or an apology or explanation. But I didn't have the energy, I wasn't smart enough.

" My Blue, I did not do anything. The instruments just started . . .behaving erratically." I could see the dials spinning in my head, giving me readings that couldn't possibly be true. " I thought maybe. . ." I would give the truth, " maybe I had made an error but I had done nothing different than on our way there or any other time." My chest and back hurt, I wanted a bed or at least a cold pack to numb the pain. " Not to sound impudent, my Blue."

" Yes, best not to do that." she curtly interjected. I quieted. We were walking away from the crash. There was no smoke here but my airways still managed one pariah couch. It took me a minute to gather any amount of motivation to speak again.

" I have been operating the skytrain since I was twelve, been doing it four years now with no supervision from my teacher Purple; I have never once had something like this occur."

She turned and her face was hardened and sad. " So what?" Her voice like brittle candy, " We're just unlucky?" The candy tasted horrible. I knew what I wanted to say but, was I brave enough to say it? She looked grief-stricken, not angry. . .oh hell, what did a dead man have left to lose?

" Luck had nothing to do with this." Her eyes widened. " I did not crash the skytrain." I dropped, got on one knee, my everything hurting at the sudden movement, I looked up to her, " But some color did, my Blue. Six years I've been operating that machine, not a single accident, not one Purple ever spoke of, Blue, this was. . ." Her eyes were so big they were bulging out of her head. She turned away. Silence fell between us. The wind rustled the branches of the nearby trees and picked up particles of dirt and chucked them vengefully. My back really did hurt, why had I decided to kneel again?

" You're saying someone. . .did this?" The candy had fallen to the sweet shop's floor and shattered. No one could enjoy it now.

" In my opinion, yes, my Blue." She turned back and there were tears in her eyes, I had expected hatred.

" Why, Purple? Why would someone do something so terrible?" I felt somewhat awkward as ridiculous as that feeling was in this situation. " I do not know, my Blu-"

" He loved me!" she pronounced and I flinched. " Why would you kill a father who loved his child?! Why would you kill a father who loved someone?!" She brought her hands to her face and started crying. My heart filled with pity even though I felt dead and I was pretty sure I hated her. I often forgot she was so young. Only fourteen. Fourteen and fatherless. I let her cry for a few moments.

" Why would you kill anyone?" I asked calmly and she stopped crying to look at me. " You get angry, and unhappy, and you hate. Or you stop caring and decide it doesn't matter. Revenge, or insanity?" She smiled somehow and wiped her eyes quickly. " It was a rhetorical question," she returned, " you fucking idiot."

Blue

I was walking through a forest. Trees, and birds, and filthy dirt. Undergrowth. The way the setting sun lit the ground in patches. Squirrels danced in the leaves, hiding upon the nearing of unusual visitors. Stumps, fallen branches, rotting leaves. Death and life in one cycling event. I've never been in a forest before. I never wanted to be in one again. Felt alone. Felt. . .empty, felt sad.

Purple

It was dark and you could feel it in the air. The sun had disappeared. Walking behind Blue was awful. She let off a blue plume of sorrow wherever she wandered and I was always in it, always fanning it away, coughing; choking on it. My back and legs hurt and it was late.

" My Blue," She didn't pause and neither did I, " perhaps we should rest for the night?" She was silent. I waited before asking, " My Blue?" again. She stopped, I halted as well. " How fast does the skytrain go?"

I blinked and couldn't remember. " Fast." I answered lamely. " How fast?!" she retorted sharply, whipping her head back. I looked down to the earth, " I am not certain exactly how fast. . ." She scowled and looked forward again. Sighing, she sat abruptly in the dirt.

" Fast I'm guessing?" Her voice sounded weak, " Father would know." She made a choking noise and it was nice to know I wasn't the only one running out of air. I sat down slowly, legs crossed, a ways behind her. I frowned over at her, " He would." I offered, as weakly as she sounded. She huffed and sighed.

" I never wanted this to happen." she said and I nodded, of course she hadn't. She looked back at me, I thought she was going to say something but she didn't. She had no words left to say. Then she looked forward again. " We will rest a few hours and then continue on our way." I nodded. We both sat there a long time, becoming the only unmoving things in the dark forest. Branches and leaves crunched around us, making me afraid of the things I could not see. Blue never looked around to try and see what made the sounds as I did. She sat frozen, as if the whole world could not touch her.

Yellow

" What is this, child?" My mother held the topaz stone to the light. " Topaz." I answered dryly. She glanced down at me and frowned, " That's wrong." she retorted. I crossed my arms over my chest. " It's topaz." She held my stare for a moment; I didn't flinch. Then a smile sprouted along her lips, " I like the confidence." I nodded, she always did. She placed the rock down, " You know you always were so smart, I can never pull anything over on you." She sat up on the table, her big, tulley dress hanging over the side.

" Not like that Blue girl, jeez she's a-" Mother patted her head, " empty one." Many people thought Mother was kind, many people were wrong. " Why don't you just court her like she wants?" Mother asked and brushed her long, voluminous hair over her shoulder. I scowled and rolled my eyes.

" What would be in it for me?"

" Ah, my sweet, that's where you've got it wrong." She fiddled with her hair in-between her fingers, " People's happiness is reward enough." I narrowed my eyes at her, she was such a liar. " And by happiness you mean. . .?" She laughed lightly and flicked her hand in my direction, " There you go with your smartness again, you get it all from me you know." She chuckled and I didn't get the joke. Who else would I get it from?

" Well, is that all?" I stated impatiently and she frowned, "

You're so unlikable, you know?" I smirked momentarily, " I get it all from you." She looked shocked a second and then grinned, " So clever." She poked my nose and I shifted away from her but smiled. I could not lie, I sometimes enjoyed my mother's and I's back and forths. As long as I was at least on equal footing. I wasn't someone who took joy in losing.

I stood up and cleared my throat, " Why would you want me to court her anyway?" I stared off at a portrait of a burning rose on a red wall. " Never said I did." she replied calmly. I tightened my hands to fists and put them in my pockets. I turned away and walked to the open window. I inhaled the cool, releasing air. Fresh like a brook. Cold like a mountain. I felt along the smooth wood frame. " You implied it." I uttered quietly, she shifted and asked, " Just don't see why you won't. A boy your age should like girls, shouldn't he?" I didn't like girls. I liked women. " Maybe. . ." I replied softly and watched the open exterior softly move, we were on the first floor of the Red Mansion. Some random study somewhere; the room hardly mattered, right?

" Don't tell me you like boys like Red does." My mother scoffed, " That would just be so unsightly." I didn't see why. Men liking men. Women liking women. All the same. Color loving color. " I don't." I stated and I heard her chuckle. " Nice, so who do you like?" I slid my hand back across the red wood nervously. " Not sure, too young to know I guess." I offered lamely. She huffed loudly, " Well, figure it out, I wanna know if I can mentally hook you up with Blue or not." I sighed. " Will do, Mother." She grinned and I heard her stand up. " Good, smart boy." she praised and then wandered from the room. I let my frame relax and held my chin in my yellow hand. I stared out to the sky, there was something different about it today.

Yellow

I sashayed out of the room. That child was always so in his head. Could spend more time thinking about a problem then it would take to solve it. But Yellow had always been like that. Part of me wondered if I had gone wrong somewhere. He was smart and could hold his own in the back-and-forth but that inability to act, that was what gave me my own cause to pause

"Yellow," It was Red, coming down the hall towards me. " Yes?" I returned, smiling widely. He had a scowl, always SO unhappy. He was taller than me, almost six foot; just a little taller than Blue. I wondered if he treasured his height or disregarded it like he did most things. " Dancing Sun Island." He had his hands on his hips as he halted across from me. I had told him I'd think about it.

" We've discussed this already." I chirped. He frowned. " I just haven't made up my mind yet." He gave a small mutter of frustration and then exclaimed, " How much time do you need, you airhead?! It's one small island!" He threw his hands out. He was wrong, it was one simple island that HE WANTED. That made a world of difference. Desire was the strongest thing to motivate a person. Wanting this, needing that, looking for. That's why my child concerned me, he didn't really 'want' anything, or maybe he did desire, and he was just good at keeping his cards close to his chest.

" It's sentimental, my dear friend. I've owned that island my whole life." Red rolled his eyes, " I doubt you've ever set foot on it."

" Well, you've never set foot in the Flame Peaks and you'd never give those up."

He huffed, " That's different; family tradition. The Reds have always owned the peaks."

" Well I've always owned that island."

He frowned and it was disheartened. Why did he want that island?

" But it hasn't been in Yellow control for as long as anyone can remember. . .The Blues owned it less than a generation ago." I shrugged and smiled, " I said I'll think about it." He crossed his arms and scowled, then turned his back to me, dejectedly. " Ok," he said softly, " Just. . .think about it." He walked away down the hall, off to do something else. I wondered what it was, perhaps something important; some business. Suddenly I thought, what if it's governing? I mean Reds have no Greens, must they run their kingdoms themselves? I smirked in amusement, now there was a scary thought.

Purple

" Wake up!" I felt a harsh impact on my side. My eyes flashed open and I took in air fast; sitting up in alarm. I blinked and looked to Blue. Her hair was messy, dirt and twigs in it. Her eyes dark and tried; it was still black outside. Her frame taunt, expression displeased. " We've rested too long, we need to go."

" Yes, my Blue." I passively agreed, I didn't overthink the fact she'd kicked me. I heard her 'tch' and she glared off as I slowly stood. " We need to get there. The mansion."

" Red's?" I asked and she glowered at me harshly. I sighed, " Red's."

" Don't speak. Gosh, you're dumb." She turned away and held the bridge of her nose. I agreed but she didn't have to be so cruel about it. I chose not to respond because it didn't look like it was a statement I was supposed to respond to, and the only respectful response would have been 'Yes, my Blue.' anyway. I waited for her feet to move, because it would have been disrespectful to walk ahead of her. Then we began to travel again. It was stupid. It was still dark; we couldn't see. We had to go much slower than we would have otherwise. I kept getting tripped up by vines and roots, and other foliage. Blue didn't trip once, I resented her more for it. Finally, I was at my limit. I was ready to say something. Speak out for once in my miserable life. Tell her what I really thought about trekking blindly through the wilderness, with the sky pitcher than my inner frustration; which I promise you had gotten quiet dark. As I finalized my decision, I heard this sound. It was. . .like a swoosh. Like a bird dropping down from its resting branch to the ground, almost soundless; almost. I looked up to Blue, who walked a good ten yards in front of me. She was bathed in moonlight, her dress, which had tears and still fresh blood stains, moved slowly in the fresh night breeze. She looked beautiful then. I looked into the shadows on the outskirts of the clearing, in which we were traveling through. Dark, untrustworthy shapes. Something felt off, I didn't know what it was but I knew it felt bad.

" My Blue?" I started and she turned. " Yes, Purple." she grunted, clearly running low on patience. " I think something is amiss." She frowned and asked, " What is?" I shifted back and forth, admitting, " I'm not certain." She scoffed and retorted, " Then why are you wasting time?!" She stamped a foot down angrily and continued, " Wasting time on stupid things! All I want to do is make it back to the Red Mansion! All I want is to be able to come back and get my father! Why do you intend on making that so difficult, Purple?!" She was screaming. But I wasn't listening. Five people had emerged from the shadows; they all wore head to toe black, ink mesh over their eyes, full masks; tall boots, gloves. They looked like warriors in a desert, although these guys looked thirsty for more than just water.

" My Blue!" I cried and ran forward. " Purple, what?!" she exclaimed, obviously distressed. I grabbed her hand and began to pull her back the way we came; my eyes glued to the strangers behind us. " Unhand me!" she hollered, pulling away.

" My Blue!"

" Let go!" She tore free and fell back. I felt all my neck hair stand up as they began to race towards us.

" Th-them!" I screamed, " Who by gosh?! Who-" She turned her head and her eyes grew wide. She jumped up, " Who are they?!" she shouted.

" I don't know!"

" Idiot! Why didn't you just say so?! Damn it!" Blue looked indecisive for a moment and then tore past me. I turned and sprinted after her. Who were these colors? What did they want from us? Were we in danger? . . .Probably?

" This way!" Blue jumped over a fallen log and I copied her. For someone who has spend her whole life in an environment where no physical exertion was required, she was quite athletic. Leaves flew up behind us, branches snapped, feat beat. I was surprisingly calm considering we were definitely being pursued. Sure my heart raced and lungs burned but well, I wasn't really fearful of capture or death or whatever these people wanted. I didn't really have any aspirations or purpose. I didn't really have a reason to stay. I was only living because it was convenient.

Only because breathing was a non-voluntary action, because it was more work to die. People say life is hard, I would like to challenge them by saying death is harder. . .

My foot got snagged on one of those damn brambles. I let out a short cry and collided with the ground. My face hit the dirt and a small pain entered the points of contact. I tried to scramble up but my foot was tangled. I looked ahead to Blue, she had stopped. She looked ahead and then back to me, eyes skittering fast; sweat pouring down her skin. She sprinted back to me, after the moment of hesitation. Wordlessly, we worked to free my foot. Then we jumped up. They were in front of us now, circled around somehow. I exchanged a glance with Blue. We wouldn't be able to outpace them now. She stepped forward bravely. " What do you want?!" The shadows of the trees draped over the pursuers' frames, making them almost invisible.

" Your head, Blue." The voice was deep and dark and muffled. Chilling. Blue didn't flinch but did look at me, she was stalling. She needed a plan. We needed a plan. They clearly could outmaneuver us here, they were lying in wait, they had every advantage; numbers, clothes that blended into the forest, a knowledge of how to maneuver without falling.

" Why?!" Blue demanded heatedly, " What score is this?!"

The figure was silent for a moment, I should have been thinking of some way to escape but I was suddenly curious myself. Why did they want to kill Blue? Why were they pursuing us? Were they responsible for the skytrain's crash?

" The score of our people. You Blues have done them wrong for generations, you and the rest of the Primaries. We will kill you and give everyone a right to choose their own path."

Their own path? I looked to Blue and she seemed upset and in thought.

" How will my murder give everyone a right to choose?" she asked and her body was as tightly pulled as violin strings.

" The Blues will disappear and then the Yellows and Reds will fight amongst each other, weakening them. Then we will push the house of cards down." Blue looked down to the ground. Her eyes were hard. Then she looked up.

" So, you're terrorists?" The group stood stick still, like stone statues, like soldiers. Like soldiers against this young girl and I.

" Revolutionaries." the dark voice replied. Blue's eyes blazed in the shadows of the forest. " So, terrorists." There was no reaction from the terrorist revolutionaries. Except the fact that blades extended down from their wrists, glinting even in the sparse light. The deep, distorted voice replied, " Whatever you say, Princess."

Blue

They ran towards us, moving into a formation like a flock of geese. The leader who had been speaking to me at the V's head. I decided to change my strategy, running hadn't worked so maybe hiding would. First I had to get past these jokers. Part of me was scared but more was determined. These were lesser colors than myself! These were fools, so violent as to carry blades and so ashamed as to hide their color. I had neither knife nor concealing cloak and I was still better than them. Like an ocean lies over sand and rock and dirt.

I dodged to the left of a blade and shoved one of them out of the way. I sprinted off, dirt flying up behind me. It was do or die. Someone reached for me, I ducked. Someone jumped for me, they missed. Oh, I was on fire, and with how mad I imagined them underneath their masks, there was plenty of steam as a result. One threw a blade, it nicked my ear. I entered this thick place of underbrush; feeling my leg muscles scream. I grit my teeth and kept going. Keep going. Keep going!

Purple

I was entirely surrounded by black cloaked killers. Sweat dropped down my forehead and I held my hands up in surrender. They had their blades pointed towards me.

" What shall we do with him?" one voice asked the leader.

" Restrain him and bind him." the dark voice answered.

Blue

I skidded to a stop. Paused. Bats flew overhead, I looked back. I wasn't being followed. I frowned. That was wrong.

Purple

I was tackled to the ground harshly, the impact with the ground being unpleasant to say the least. Two of the assassins grabbed my arms and two others my legs. A scream died in my throat. It was a nightmare, looking up at the masks of dark, featureless attackers. I would never know the eyes that killed me.

Blue

My left? My right? I looked back to where I had fled from. Purple. . .

Purple

The tear of my black vest and white undershirt was quick and brief. I screamed now, what were they going to do with me?! One of them, maybe the leader, maybe not, put a shoe on my bare chest. Their sole was a soft leather, scratched and cold.

" Please, I don't want any part of this!" I pleaded, tears forming in my eyes. I struggled; feverish yet fruitless.

Blue

Purple! my mind screamed, you left him! Of course that idiot couldn't escape by himself! I looked back and felt hesitation. I wanted to save him. Who knows? He could already be dead. . .excuses! " Your head, Blue." The timbre of the voice echoed in every corner of my mind. It made my skin grow goosebumps like warts. I was afraid. As much as I missed him. . .I did not want to join my father. I'm sorry, Dad. I dubiously began to retrace my steps.

Purple

" This will free you."; the voice of the terrorist above me, not the leader. They began to chant. I looked around in a panic, all the others had their heads bowed; their grip was stronger than a mountain lion's claws in a carcass. I looked back up and the chant was fast like a prayer, made of sounds I could not even begin to understand. Suddenly a pain like a hot poker on the inside began, I cried out, arching my back in an attempt to escape it.

Blue

That was Purple's screaming. My feet got a little less dubious. My pace got faster.

Purple

" My Blue!" I cried out because I didn't know what else to do. I didn't know who else to call out to. I didn't know anything. Primaries, it HURT!

Blue

And a little faster. My hair flew out behind me like a kite in the wind. Purple! He was all I had left, sure I knew Yellow and Red but Purple lived with me, he was there in so many of my memories; usually to the side cleaning or taking orders but he was there, and I've just recently realized how valuable that is.

Purple

Some laughed at me. " My Blue?" one repeated in amusement. " Why is he calling out to her?" I screamed and collapsed down with a half cry-half whimper. My insides contorted and spun; ripping apart. The chant continued above me; sounded like a machine malfunctioning in rhythm.

Blue

I came close enough so I could see them. Purple was thrashing on the ground, four of the terrorists holding him down. One stood with a foot on his chest, looking down at him. It didn't make sense, first-what were they DOING to him?! He looked to be in serious distress, he didn't have a shirt on, and anyway, I thought they were after me. 'Your head, Blue.' and all. I needed to be smart about this, I was outnumbered, didn't have any weapons, and was an assassination target. I shook the fear from my head and crept forward, keeping my body lowered. I started to quietly circle the area which held them, so I could hide behind one of the trees. Purple wailed and screamed and I hid behind an old sycamore.

" Stockholm syndrome?" Left Arm offered to Right Leg. I didn't know what they were talking about. " Don't laugh." Right Arm barked, " Don't you know what they do to Secondaries?! They're born and the first thing they hear is how they are supposed to serve the Primaries until they die! Isn't that disgusting?" I thought this was ironic to say while torturing the color you pitied so much. I watched the fabric of Right Arm's mouth move while they spoke. I wondered what color lips those hypocritical words came from. The one standing on Purple was speaking some kind of chant. Their weapons were seemingly attached to their gloves, hard to snatch; smart. My eyes quickly scanned the ground for a weapon. I spotted a rock about the size of my palm. I picked it up and felt my blood pulse wildly in my ears. Do or die. I threw it overhead at the terrorist on top of Purple. There was a thud and a curse interpreted their chant. It hit their shoulder. I slammed my back to the tree, hiding quickly. I admit I was near hyperventilation.

" The hell was that?!" Left Arm announced.

" A stone." Leader answered. 'Your head.' I shivered.

" Who-?"

" Who else?!" Right Leg snapped, " It's the damn Primary!" I heard movement.

" Hey! Don't let go!"

" But she's right out there! Let's find her and kill her!"

" Patience, Rosa." Leader again, " If Miss Blue would like to watch us bind Purple then she may."

" But Boss!"

" No buts!" I heard Right Leg squat back down and then some cracking?! Screaming?! What?! I stuck my head out again and saw Purple on top of one of the terrorists! He punched them violently and my eyes widened in surprise. My Purple? Attacking someone?

" Don't you fucking touch her! Don't you fucking touch me!" he screamed and they drug him off the one he had tackled. " Purple, please!" It was Right Arm again. " We are going to free you!"

" Fuck you!" Tears rolled down his face and his expression was this anguished anger I had never seen before. " I don't want to be free!" He kicked out violently and they worked to restrain him once more, I brought my head back and covered my mouth. What should I DO?! I didn't want to die! I didn't want to get hurt! I didn't want to take those risks! They obviously weren't going to kill him, they would have done so already if that was the case. They were going to 'bind' him, whatever that was. I felt a choking tension in my chest and my eyes sprouted tears. But I didn't want him to be in pain. But it was me or him. I-I was the ocean! I couldn't die here! I covered my mouth to crush a sob to silence. I had made my choice. . .

Purple

The chant began again. I cried out and their hands were as powerful as before. I had only been able to break free because one of the ones holding my legs had let go. Didn't know why, something about a rock. The tearing at my guts was so bad, I could focus on little else. Noises began to blur together and lose their distinction that made them different from one another, all joined my screams in a mess of sound that brewed and gurgled in my ears. I wanted to die, because at least then this pain would stop. Then again maybe death would be worse, maybe it would just be this forever; ceaseless pain. If I was dying right now I would not know how I felt about it. Perhaps I deserved it, some sin of mine finally catching up to me, or maybe I was innocent. It did not matter in the end, no one deserves this. No sinner or Saint. I wanted Blue and teacher and my bedroom, I wanted to scale the outside of the Red Mansion, and be mocked by Yellow and Blue, I wanted to man the skytrain, to cook steak and season it just the way Blue liked it, to dust the blue china in the one long hall on the third floor; never realized I liked such things before. Maybe I did not and I would just prefer anything juxtaposed to this agony. Tears poured down my face like blood rushing from an open wound and I screamed like I would never be heard.

Plasma

" He passed out." I informed quietly, looking down at Purple's now sleep-like face.

" Thank Primaries!" Rosa exclaimed dramatically, rolling his head around his neck, " That screaming was grating on my nerves."

" Rosa." Leader warned and I sighed and shook my head disapprovingly. We were not supposed to use the Primaries as curses. Leader was adamant on the fact that they were colors just like us. Noble families, greedy and cruel enough to subjugate and conquer, but colors nonetheless. Not gods, not a higher species, just people; just colors.

" So," I began, looking to Leader. " She's watching us right now?" They nodded, " Assuredly." I looked out to the dark shadows of the surrounding trees.

" She could be laying a trap for us." I worried aloud, Rosa and Dantalion were looking at me as I spoke. " Unlikely." Leader answered and stood up, " She doesn't know where we are going. She's just a child, not smart enough to set a trap; doesn't have the resources or ingenuity." Turquoise was near done the binding ritual. I stood up, Rosa and Dantalion followed my lead, " So . .

." Rosa stated after a moment of silence, " we hunt her down now?" I looked and Leader replied, " There's no need, she's within earshot of us. She'll come out when she's ready."

" What?!" Rosa exclaimed and me and Dantalion exchanged a nervous glance. " If we pursue her, she'll run off again." Leader explained and Rosa growled, " Then we'll catch her."

" Maybe." Leader returned, " Or we'll lose her. She'll hide and we'll search all night, fruitless."

I imagined Leader was a man beneath their mask. I imagined them in heavy clothes of a rich dark shade of blue, n-not Primary blue of course. . .ugh, my admiration for their shades was entrenched so deep! But a different hue, maybe a deep, dark scarlet, or a light, pretty yellow- he could be anything, but he was my hero no matter who and what he was under that mask. I knew I would follow him. I knew that from the first moment I saw him. His intelligence, his deep, rich voice, everything about him.

" Right now, she watches us. She will remain near, and eventually she will provide us an opening. She'll expose herself and give us our chance." Leader informed. Rosa looked to

Dantalion and I could tell they didn't understand. I didn't either but I didn't care. I would follow him until my legs gave out and my bones decayed; I was in love with this man.

Red

" Piece of shit!" I exclaimed and shoved all of the garbage off my desk. It clattered to the floor and I turned around quickly.

" Purple!" I called out vehemently, she responded, " Yes, my Red?" formally in reply. She stood, hands behind her straight back; standing to the left of my open door. " I need a cigar!" She nodded and crossed the red polished wooden floor. She squatted down and picked up an unused cigar from the floor. I blushed slightly as I took it from her. It had been right there in front of me.

" Here you go, my Red." she stated and I frowned, " My lighter?" She reached down into one of her proper vest pockets and pulled it out. She handed it to me with a calm smile. I scowled and fell back into my puffy red seat. It rolled back slightly with my weight and I brought the lighter up and lit my cigar, which I held between my teeth. I looked to my cleared desk and then the disastrous pile of important papers and useful tools on the floor. I groaned outright and rested my heavy head in one of my large hands.

" Something amiss, my Red?" Purple asked politely. I looked to her miserably and her calm, content countenance did not change. I didn't want to confide in the help, didn't want to be reduced to that. I exhaled some rich smoke and glanced down to the mess. " Yellow." I muttered and she nodded. " What has she done?" Purple responded in a sympathetic tone. I looked up to her, she looked respectfully understanding, she made it so easy to be weak.

" Dancing Sun Island." I explained. She hummed, knowing exactly what I was talking about. I looked to my tall study's window, but couldn't see out; for it was covered in heavy satin curtains." She won't give it to me." I complained, shuffling a hand through my hair; I didn't want it to sound like I was whining.

" Perhaps you could offer her something in exchange for it? The Pluto region has never been overly useful to you." I looked to her and rearranged the position of my cigar slightly. " An island isn't worth a whole region," I retorted and took a drag, " As useless as Pluto is." She laughed gently. " I suppose so, perhaps you could offer something smaller?" I groaned and leaned back, letting my head hang over the back of my chair. " That's not the problem! She hasn't brought up trade, Purple, I can't!" I sat back up and exhaled some more smoke, hunching forward. " I'll seem desperate, see?" I placed my hands together and stared at them in thought, " The problem is I don't have anything she. . .wants." Purple nodded and placed a finger to her chin. " Well, what does she want?" I tried to relax my body by leaning back. " That's the problem with Yellow, you never know what she wants."

" Oh." Purple replied quietly, there was a quiet and I exhaled some more unpleasant smoke. " Maybe she doesn't want anything?" Purple suggested dubiously. I turned in my luxurious swiveling chair, " Everyone wants something." I paused my seat's rotation as it reached my servant again. Her expression was sullen.

" What do you want, my Red?" she asked with a frail quality. I blew out some more smoke. " Currently?" I replied, " Dancing Sun and Blue's ass." Purple cracked a grin and looked to the floor, " You are quite fond of him, aren't you, my Red?" I shrugged carelessly but was helpless to keep a smile from my face.

" I'm fond of that body." I whistled exaggeratedly; Purple chuckled softly and blushed. " W-well, I'm glad you enjoy his company, my Red." she replied, trying to be formal but looking a little flustered. Finally something to ruffle that composed, perfect exterior. She was always unsure of how to act when I talked about my attraction to Blue, honestly I talked about it a surprising amount. Not on purpose, it just always. . .came up?

" Anyway, that color's a mystery, always has been." I stated easily, referring to Yellow and leaning my chin into my hand, " I've known her since childhood and I could tell you maybe two true facts about her." Purple blinked widely, " Only two?" I nodded. She cocked head to the side, " What are they?" I puffed on my cigar.

" She's yellow and a bitch." Purple laughed lightly. That color had a weird sense of humor, I was being entirely serious. I frowned at her and she quickly stopped laughing. " Well, I wish you good luck with the island and with Yellow," she started off towards the door, " I recommend you get to bed soon."

" Why?" I retorted, it was still early in the night.

" Countenance." Purple answered, pausing her stride, " Do you still wish me to wake you?" I gave a scowl, stupid Yellow traditions. Who wanted to eat a pastry at two am?! " I had forgotten all about it." I confessed and Purple chirped, " So, I shall be waking you?"

" Precisely, my dear." I replied and spun my chair again. Purple nodded and then began to make her way to the door again. " Oh!" I exclaimed suddenly, an idea striking me. She halted, " Yes, my Red?"

" Make all the treats yellow tonight." Her eyes widened and she looked horrified, " All of them?" she questioned, looking fearful. I stopped my chair's spin and stared at her, a grin stretching my mouth.

" Oh, you heard what I said." I replied coyly. She paled and bowed, " Yes, as you wish, my Red." she returned solemnly. I exhaled some more smoke from my cigar and didn't lose my smirk. That island was going to be completely and utterly mine.

Blue

I grit my teeth and felt a biting anger in my chest, they were talking about their strategy so openly! They didn't see me as any kind of threat, did they?! Ignorant, disrespectful swine! I would make them pay! First with their lives, then with everything they stood for! They were waiting for me to give them an opening?!

How impudent! I would give them an opening alright. One they would never forget!

" Well, that took a shorter amount of time than expected." Leader announced as I stepped out into their view. I started walking towards them and forced my expression to a saddened one. I had no weapons. Nothing to use against them. Wrong! Who's been telling you lies? I've had years of training, behaving this way, that way; gathering reactions and nonreactions; expressions and tone. I was not an actress but a detective, I could tell when father would sway and when he would not. I could tell when Red was displeased and when he was very displeased. I could tell when Yellow was tolerating me and when he was so ready to find a new hiding spot. I was now a police commissioner in an interrogation room, ready to pull all the information I needed from the suspected criminal across from me. Only one tiny problem, this leader terrorist had a mask on, that, for me at least, was like walking into a hostage situation blindfolded.

" I want to speak to you, not on hostile terms. . ." I gripped my hands down by my sides and tried to make my face as emotional as possible while still being believable. " What is the topic of discussion?" Leader replied calmly and Rosa? I think that's what their name was, not that it mattered, exclaimed, " What?! Let's seize her!"

" What is the topic?" Leader repeated, looking to me. His soldier silenced, looking to me as well. Purple laid on the ground at their feet, looking worse for wear. There was something wrong with his bare chest but it was so odd, I couldn't mentally process it for now; I put it away for later.

" My Purple." I stated and one terrorist, the pretentious one, scoffed, " He's not 'yours'." they spat. I looked to Leader, " I am willing to negotiate."

" What do you have to trade?" he responded, at least I guessed it was a he-deep voice. " Information. I know the other Primaries' locations, habits, schedules. I can tell you what you need to know in order to plan another attack."

" Another?" he questioned and I narrowed my eyes, " I'm not an idiot. I know you killed my father." I hardened my expression. I had to keep my emotions out of this. Revenge would come, just not now. " The Skytrain was sabotaged by you." I finished. The terrorists were silent, then their leader probed, " Why is the information more valuable than your life?"

I had an answer. " I am but a child. Red and Yellow hold significantly more power than myself. You said you planned to make them fight amongst each other, well they will do that whether I am dead or not; a child is not a worthy adversary. They will walk all over me. Information on them would be much more valuable than my life, or lack thereof." Leader thought this over and then reminded, " Your Purple?" His side of the deal.

" I want him and safe passage for both of us, you and your colors will not attack us until we reach the Red Mansion." One of the subordinate terrorists whispered to another. There was quiet muttering until Leader nodded his head, " Ok. I'm glad you realize how little you matter." The dark voice got under my skin. He had NO idea. I was the ONLY thing that mattered, I was the ocean! Because of my blue skin I would always-always be better than this color! I would always be better than this man, better than everyone!

" First the information." he ordered. " First Purple." I returned, " Once he lays beside my feet, I will tell you all I know." Before he could challenge me, I added, " I cannot outpace you while carrying an unconscious body." He nodded and stated, " Dantalion, carry Purple over to Blue."

One of the terrorists, Dantalion, looked to Purple on the ground and then back to their leader. Then they took a step towards him only to have a different terrorist block them with an arm. " Leader, Dantalion, wait. We can't just hand him over to 'her'!" They threw an arm out to me. " We can't send him back to a static, hopeless life of servitude! We must free him. That's what we're here to do." They looked down to Purple. " That's why we're here. . ." I narrowed my eyes, the deal was off if I didn't get him. The terrorists' leader's blade extended with a small sliding sound. It happened quickly with efficiency. My eyes widened because I couldn't help it, it was shocking, what happened. He stabbed them. Right in the gut; quickly. Blink and you would have missed it.

There was this still shock a moment and then, " Plasma!" One, I think Rosa, screamed. They caught the one who had been stabbed, a light purplish gray-white running down through their dark clothing. They looked down, seemingly shocked, and then looked back to Leader, " Why? I was so loyal to you."

" Plasma! Oh my Primaries! Are you ok?!" the one who grabbed the victim shouted. Leader looked to Dantalion and they quickly snatched up Purple and nearly running over to me, placed him down roughly. I reached back and felt the rock in my pocket. Cold sweat ran down my neck. My plan. . .WOULDN'T WORK! It was simple, I'd bash the head of whoever brought me Purple, maybe even Leader himself, knocking them unconscious. I could take a hostage and have leverage. I'd force them to leave me alone and wait for Purple to awake, then we'd be able to carry the live terrorist all the way to the Red Mansion, but Leader, whoever this murder was, had thrown my whole plan out the window! It wouldn't work! This guy had just stabbed one of his own subordinates, unless they had some long-lasting feud I was unaware of, over something small! They would let me kill Dantalion. No heart, no hostage. I put my hand back down by my side. I needed a new plan. It felt like there were rocks in my throat. Dantalion quickly returned to the group.

" Leader!" Rosa called, they had slumped to the ground with Plasma in their lap. " We need to get them medical attention!"

" We don't give fools who question orders medical attention." Leader coldly replied. " Leader, what?! Please!" Rosa pleaded with indignance. " Unless you wish to join them I suggest you stand up." Rosa was warned. The air was so tense and horrible, it was awful. These were disgusting lesser terrorists that had a hand in my father's killing and yet-. . .the way Rosa looked between his fallen comrade and his leader. Dantalion looked down at them and Rosa's tense frame relaxed. " I think I will stay down here with them." Dantalion looked away and Rosa produced a guttural sound as his neck was slashed. I looked away in horror, feeling my heart pound uncontrollably. I wanted to vomit, I wanted to vomit! It was disgusting, the sound of their throat and the blood, one body slumping on top of another. Plasma gave a weak cry. I looked back and could not take the tears from my eyes. I would see that for the rest of my life.

" Thank you, Turquoise." Leader praised stoically and then looked to me. " Why so distressed, Blue?" he asked, almost mockingly. " A little bit of justice should feel nice, shouldn't it?" Bile. Bile! Coming up my throat. Vomit. Vomit! Not in front of him. I swallowed it down. The tears and cold air stung my eyes.

" By my hand, yes. By a hand they trusted?"

" Spare the morality speech, just got rid of those with Plasma." I shook my head no. Why? I was just complaining to Dad on the skytrain, why? Why couldn't he have said yes to staying the night?! If he had, he would still be alive right now. . .

" The information, our deal. Don't make me regret my decision."
I nodded and swallowed back more vomit. " Yes." I said, "
Getting there." I cleared my throat full of disgusting matter and
began, " The Yellows have an odd tradition called countenance,
it take place at around two am and it is when they awake from
slumber to eat treats. The Reds wake up later than most,
sometimes not till ten am and stay awake later as a result. The
Red Mansion has five floors with useless rooms on everyone of
them. The Reds sleep on the fourth floor. The Yellow Manor has
three floors and hallways like labyrinths, it's more expansive in
terms of how wide it is. They sleep on the second floor. Reds are
traditionally temperamental, tight knit, while Yellows are
traditionally more independent and logical. . .You are more
likely to catch a Yellow alone." My body filled with dread at the
thought of Leader and his band of terrorists breaking into one of
Yellow's peaceful sitting areas, interrupting my love's quiet
contemplation. Heh. I wonder what he thinks about in those
fancy chairs. Those Blue, Yellow, and Red chairs. Looking out
the window. What is he always looking for?

I couldn't lie though and give fake information as much as I
would like to. If they had already collected any data on Primary
behavior and my words contradicted that. Bye-bye, Blue.

" What about their language?" Leader asked and I blinked widely. " Apparently same as you." I informed.

" I meant slang, titles?" What weird information to inquire about? I thought he wanted to kill them, not join their book club.

" All Primaries call each other by their color, 'Blue', 'Yellow', 'Red', servants call them, 'my Blue', 'my Yellow', so on. The parent Primary traditionally calls their offspring, 'my child'."

" Wait, so you and your father were both called Blue?" Leader responded and I made an expression of confusion. " . . .Um, yes." Leader exchanged a look with Turquoise, who was wiping dark pink blood off their blade with a black rag. My spine shivered. " Odd." he commented casually. Strangest terrorists ever. " That will be all, Blue." he said and then added, " Get out of here now. Before I change my mind." I leaned down slowly and felt strange and shaken and scared. I also just couldn't stop staring at the star of turquoise imprinted upon Purple's chest.

Yellow

The sun had finally set. Its reds and yellows and oranges disappeared under the contours of the peaks. I had watched it go. I brought one of my ankles to sit upon my opposing knee and thought about how the colors blended together and made the sky pink and orange. It was breathtaking.

" My Yellow," A calm voice greeted me from the door, " It's about time for bed, do you not think so?"

" Did Mother ask you to fetch me?" A small silence, then a placid laugh. " Yes, you always know. How do you do that?" I looked over to Green, she wore a long, white dress; plain and loose. Her hair was long and braided relaxedly. She was less voluptuous than mother. In fact, she looked much like a tall girl who had been climbing a tree, and stayed in the branches so long- the leaves stained her skin their color.

" It is obvious. You've never been the babysitting type, you only check in on my well-being when Mother asks that of you." She laughed softly. " Well, I suppose that's true but that's not because I don't ca-"

" It's fine." I stood up. " Please escort me to my bedroom." Yellows don't have Purples because Purples, true ones at least, have no yellow in them. I often fantasized about having one around the house when I was younger. She was kind and gentle and attractive. Though I don't know how I would deal with one in reality if Blue's Purple is anything to go by. Our Green fulfills some chores of a Purple because we don't have one but Green's a Green, through and through. You can just tell.

We wandered through the hall and ascended to the third floor by marble staircase. The guest floor was adorned as everything else, Red was into bling. Into jewels and shiny things. We were walking across the red wood when I stopped. Mother's room. A shiny red door. I wonder if she locked it. When I was ten, I got my own room right beside her. I had been thrilled then, now I wasn't quite sure if it was preferable. The quiet was nice but little else.

" My Yellow?" Green paused and looked back to me. I looked to her and her expression turned slightly concerned. " Something a matter?"

" I shall sleep in your chambers tonight." I stated and her face showed surprise. " Uh-oh-a-" she stuttered for a moment and then nodded quickly, " Of course, please follow me." Her room was a few rooms away from our own, so we could have easy access to our servants and yet they could have the useless space to remind them of their place. Green's door was red. She opened it quickly and held it for me. I entered and looked around.

Smaller than my room, with a beige ceiling and brown wood flooring. It was rectangular, with a small box window currently masked by a simple white curtain. There was a white desk adjacent to a queer bed of purple, orange, and green bedding. There was a full brown bookshelf beyond it. Papers, scrolls, books, and quills were spilled over the desk and their contents extended even to the bed. After Green shut the door, she quietly hurried over and cleared the bed, looking quite flustered.

" I'm so sorry about the mess, my Yellow:" Green apologized profusely, " I, you see, was not expecting company."

" You work even here." I stated and she turned to me with surprise, " Oh, um, yes, my Yellow." She awkwardly grinned, " Unfortunately the day to day squabble of running a kingdom does not vanish at our bi-weekly visitations." She had some sweat on her face as she set the stack of bills and tax reports on the crowded desk. She was nervous, but anyone could tell that.

" I did not realize it was so much paperwork." I informed and she laughed uneasily, " What did you think I did in my room all day?" I shrugged and sat down on her bed. " Not sure, didn't think too hard over it." Her face softened and she said, " It's ok, I wouldn't in your position either." She turned to me, leaning her derriere on the desk. " Tell me." I prompted, turning my whole face to her, " What do you think the purpose of life is?" She was obviously startled.

" My Yellow?" she questioned with wide eyes. " W-why would you ask that?" My eyes grew fierce, " Why aren't the rest of you asking that? Are you content to wander through life with no final destination? With no end point? Why do we endure the petty struggles and harsh realities?" Her countenance turned sad, " My Yellow, are you ok?" I laid back on her bed and stared up to the ceiling. Beige? Why would anyone make a ceiling that color? Why would anyone make a ceiling yellow? Why would anyone make a ceiling?

" Answer me, Green." Out of my peripheral vision, she shifted. " I've been told my propose is to effectively run the Yellow kingdom, with the strong and clear aim to maintain Yellow control, while executing Yellow will and authority." I blinked and listened to her carefully. That made sense I suppose. " . . . But that's not what I believe." I turned my head to her, surprised. Her gaze was serious. " Please do not take this as an offense but. . ." She stopped and it took almost ten seconds for her to restart, " I believe the purpose of life is to find meaning in the things you do. To be appreciative of small actions and objects. To find meaning in the meaningless." I blinked widely at her and she sweated harshly and looked away to the ceiling. " B-but I could be wrong of course." I felt a smile find myself and my cheeks scrunched into hard, dense spheres, as they do.

" That's fascinating." I said and she looked back to me. " Uh, thank you." she quickly replied and then stuttered, " W-what do you think it is?" I blinked at her, my smile fading. " I don't know, that's why I asked."

" Oh!" she exclaimed, " Right! Of course. . ." My smile returned and I looked back to the ceiling, " I like your idea though, romantic." She chuckled, " Thank you, my Yellow. . ."

There was a silence for maybe a minute. " May we have sex now?" She chuckled again and reminded, " You're the one in power." I looked to her and said, " Green, I respect you. If you refuse, then I will accept that." She still looked nervous. " I've been told the answer to a Primary's request is always yes." I sat up and hunched forward, " But do you believe that?" She blinked widely and brought a hand to her chest. " N-no. . ." She looked away as if she had confessed a dreadful sin. " Then ask yourself do I wish to sleep with this color?"

" And if the answer is no?"

" Then it is so." She looked down to her bare toes. Green never wore shoes. Blue's Green wore shoes. We all wore shoes. I never bothered to ask why she did not. What an odd thing. No shoes? What could possibly be the benefit of that?

" Then no thank you. . ." she mumbled quietly and I nodded, that was fine by me, although I clearly wanted it; I had asked. " Alright." I leaned down and slipped my shoes off my feet, revealing wool yellow socks.

" My Yellow?" she asked questioningly and I looked to her calmly as I began to unbutton my jacket. " My Yellow?!" she repeated, clearly thinking I had refused her refusal. " I said I was sleeping in your chambers, I wasn't lying." I laid back on her bed after tossing my jacket to the floor. I stretched my arms over my head and said, " Turn off the lights when you are ready to go to bed. I'm ready to sleep. See you at countenance." I heard silence, then a little chuckle. " Of course, my Yellow." The lights went dark in a few minutes.

Blue

The sky was pitch and silent. Stars twinkled brightly but they brought me no inspiration. There was no beauty in the black sky, it had taken the blue day sky away. . .I missed the blue sky. A tear found my eye. Where was he?

Something moved and my eyes widened large as china plates. I jumped to see what it was! Purple groaned and blindly groped the ground in front of him. He was lying about twelve feet away from me, face in the dirt. I had drug him a ways to a secluded grove of trees. I had then tucked him under some wild roots that had decided to reach for that wicked dark sky and attempt to caress the night clouds.

" Idiot. You're awake. Took you long enough." He groaned, bringing a hand to his head and digging it into his scalp. " I nearly died trying to save you! How dare you put me in a situation where I could have been hurt?! Idiot!" Attacking Purple made me feel better, I have no idea why but, at least it was something normal, something low-stakes. Something that couldn't result in death. Rosa's blood slurping from their throat, I shuddered. Purple would never see that. He MADE me see that, see it alone. I would torture him for that fact.

" My Blue?" he said questioningly, pushing himself slowly up with his thick forearms. His back hit the roots and he turned to observe them with fright. He sighed. " My Blue, what happened?" he asked, crawling out from under them. " My head hurts. . ." he mumbled.

" Boo-hoo!" I spat sarcastically. " I had to drag a man almost double my weight through a dark forest roaming with killers!" I scowled and crossed my arms over my chest before standing up from my stump chair, berating Purple while sitting just felt wrong.

" What?" he responded dumbly and I stamped my foot down angrily. " I saved you!" He made an expression of stunned confusion. " Why?. . ." he asked cause he was stupid. I felt tears find my eyes, " Does it matter, you idiot?!" He looked suddenly uncomfortable. " Idiot!" I screamed and was breathing heavily. I realized my tears had begun to leak from my eyes so I sniffled and rubbed my arm across my face to hopefully cleanse it. I sighed and slumped back down on my stump. Never mind, I'd sit. Purple was quiet for a moment and then walked beside me before kneeling down. He asked, " Are you alright, my Blue?" My tears were fat and my posture was hunched and deflated like a dead, popped balloon.

" Purple!" I whined and Purple blinked widely, looking like an out of place dog in a high tree. I held my arms out and ordered, "

Hug me!" The misfortunate dog looked horribly regretful. "
O-ok." he said and awkwardly leaned forward, slowly wrapping
his arms around my back. I looked down at his purple back, I
could see the outline of his spinal column and his shoulder
blades. . .I grabbed him so tightly and buried my head in his
skin! I sobbed loudly and couldn't control myself anymore. " My
dad's dead! He's dead!" I cried. I kept repeating realities but I
don't know if he could understand me through the tears. They
poured in an endless stream. " By Colors, he's dead! I love him
and he's DEAD!"

Purple

I didn't know what happened with the terrorists. I didn't know
how Blue freed me or what damage had been done. As Blue
wept, it hardly mattered, I decided. I held her and she was small
and lithe, taller than me because of our current positioning. . . I
didn't know if she trusted me, and that was why she was taking
comfort from me, or if she was just desperate. Maybe I was just
as desperate. I slowly tightened my hold on her and pushed my
nose and mouth into her hair. This-this, was therapeutic. This
was orgasmic! Jeez, Blue. I felt myself getting emotional. This
was so complicated and convoluted. So dumb! I held this girl
under these stars, under this tree. This. . .maybe this. . .no. . .just
this. I'd ruin it with words.

Green

I could not sleep. My mind swirled with ideas and questions; restless. I turned my head to my left, I was lying on my bed in the Red Mansion. Yellow, the young one, was peacefully sleeping. Yellow eyelashes softly touched the cheeks of his sleeping face. He was laying on his back, head slumped along the orange pillow towards me. He wore a fancy yellow shirt that looked stiff and uncomfortable, it was crumpled now with the bedding. He hadn't even changed into nightclothes. . . I looked back to my ceiling and my tongue felt like a foreign object in my mouth. I rubbed some sweat from my forehead and wondered if changing into my bedclothes was the right move. They were quite warm.

I looked back at Yellow and I wasn't sure how I felt. In my head, he was still a child, I was made when his mother was still quite young. He wanted to sleep with me? I didn't understand it. Even more peculiar perhaps was that I had denied him and he respected that? How impudent of myself. . . I turned my body towards him and brought a green hand up before my face, to stare at it. It looked so strange in front of the yellow. I never really looked at myself. I braided my hair as not to look disorderly but I didn't ever stare in the mirror. Hardly made eye-contact with it actually. He has called my idea 'romantic'. Like a painting or a song, like the way I thought of bumblebees or wind chimes. Something different and amusing. How it hurt to be made light of. I never considered how those wind chimes felt.

Then again wasn't that all my idea was, an idea to be mused with? I had no proof. How do you proof the purpose of life? Of your own life? I looked to him and he looked at peace. I envied him. He asked about my view of life so calmly, so casually. He explained himself with such assurance, he said everything with confidence; as if he had never once been questioned. My life is always questions; lower taxes here? Fund this public works? Raise the draft age? Lower it? Yellow wants this; how do I get it? Where is it? When do I have to get it by? I sighed and gently fisted my hand. To find meaning in the meaningless. . . That's what's I told him but, my eyes searched his placid, sleeping face. What if you can't find it? My purpose of life puts the purpose of your existence in your hands, you have to appreciate the small factors, you have to find meaning, if you can't. . .that leaves only two outcomes. Either you missed out on the meaning, because you were too busy with the daily hustle and bustle to find it, or because you never invented meaning. . .you never had any. What a sad thought. That our meaning is nothing more than that of a bee's or wind chimes'. I do not want to be wind chimes . . . A green tear slipped from my left eye onto the purple sheet. I wiped it quickly. How ridiculous was I being, it was late and I was acting and feeling irrationally, that was all. Though I knew that to be true. . .my chest did not feel any lighter. It felt like it was full of rocks; rock with even less importance than wind chimes.

Blue

Thank goodness I finally forced myself to stop crying. That was SO EMBARRASSING. And while hugging Purple?! Ew! Ew! Disgusting! I stood and Purple also stood, he was staring down at his chest. He was board for a teen and completely hairless which I found a bit funny. Then again my father and Red were also hairless so maybe the men's chest hair in those books I had read had been deeply exaggerated. Purple had been silent for about a minute and looked like he was having a panic attack. Couldn't really blame him. It was certainly freaky. A star with six points and completely turquoise sat on his chest. I had touched it before he had awoken. It wasn't paint or a sticker, it was part of his skin and that was slightly terrifying. Purple was supposed to be purple after all. When he finally looked up, I stated, " The terrorists did that to you. They called it binding or something." He looked sad and pathetic. He frowned, looking back down, running his fingers over it.

" I can't feel it."

" You can't?" I replied. That was kind of weird, wasn't it part of him? " I can't." he repeated, " I feel something but it's not my hand." I looked to the turquoise star with confusion.

" What can you feel?" He gave an unhappy yet stunned look, " Fabric or something soft." His face looked deep in thought, " I didn't know you could do that to somebody else." I gave an awkward shrug. " Me neither." We fell into silence.

" So," I stated, looking around, " we need to find our way to the mansion again." He made eye-contact with me as I explained, " I lost my sense of direction in all the running."

" What about the terrorists?" Purple asked, fear evident on his face.

" I made an agreement with their leader."

" What?!" he exclaimed, " What did you trade?"

 I frowned, " Information on the Primaries."

" You sold them out?" he asked in disbelief.

" It was my life or theirs." I answered defensively, face contorting into something ugly, " What did you want me to do?!" He averted his eyes and shrugged.

" That's what I thought, you dunderhead. Now, we need to find a high place so I can pick out the direction of the mansion."

" You probably won't be able to see it." he retorted placidly, I looked to him with a harsh gaze. I didn't like the fact he was questioning me.

" Why do you say that?"

" The Red Mansion is atop a high plateau, in the center of it. We won't be able to see it, even if we climb the highest tree in this forest. We're in the wooded valley below the plateau." I sighed, " Really?"

" Really." I paused before I scowled and kicked a nearby small rock, " Well fuck!" I exclaimed, frustration growing. " How am I supposed to know where we're going?!" Purple shifted and brought his hands together in front of himself. He rubbed them nervously. " You don't know."

I looked to him with anger, why was that idiot pointing out MY flaws?! It's not like- " But I do." . . . " You do?!"

" Of course!" he replied, " You think I wouldn't remember landmarks?! I watch from the control room, the skytrain runs-ran- pre-set courses but I watched to make sure everything stayed the way it should. We've gone along this track more times than I can count. How do you not remember the surrounding area?" I crossed my arms over my chest. " Um, I wasn't paying attention I guess. It's not like I ever had to. . ." Purple shrugged and it was quiet for a minute before I pressed, " So if I can get you up high, you can show us the way to Red's?" He nodded and I sighed, " Ok. Do you want me to find a hill or something or are you-" The rest of my statement before I was rudely interrupted was 'ok with climbing a tree?'.

" On a condition." I blinked at him and physically recoiled. " What?" I asked in a shocked, bewildered voice. He shuffled in place and looked down to the floor. " I said I have a condition, two actually." I blinked widely, mouth hanging a bit open. . . " How DARE you?!" I shouted and he flinched, " You are unworthy to give me orders, you miserable Purple! I saved you and I'm your better! You should be more than happy to serve me in any way possible, and you will do so without any protest or condition!"

" You haven't even heard what they are yet." he stated in a voice that sounded like he was trying to be firm but came out only as meek.

" IT DOES NOT MATTER! WHAT YOUR CONDITIONS ARE! YOU DO NOT GET CONDITIONS!"

Some tears bubbled up in his eyes out of distress and indignance or whatever else. " That's not fair! It's not fair, you're so mean, my Blue!" I rolled my eyes, " Everyone has their place, Purple." I stopped shouting because clearly he was getting upset. " Well I never asked for this place!" he cried, Purple tears spilling down his cheeks. " I never wanted it!" He brought his hands up and wiped at his face. " Stop crying." I said dryly, he had no reason to cry.

" Y-you just cried!" he protested, voice becoming croak-like. I sighed, " Well my father's dead. You're just being a baby."

" A baby who can geumtcha. . ."

" What?" I said, grit teeth showing. " A baby who can get you-"
I stared at him harshly, daring him to finish his sentence. He
frowned, sniffled, cleared his throat; sighed. He looked to the
ground.

" Sorry, my Blue. Let's just pretend that didn't happen. I'll
cooperate." I nodded. Good.

" So," I stated strongly, " do you need me to find a hill or are
you going to climb a tree?"

Purple

I hauled myself up to the next branch, my foot pushing off
Blue's laced hands. My foot landed overtop of a small, odd
bump in the tree's bark and I pushed up even further. Some
leaves and branches scraped my back as I moved up. I missed
my fucking shirt. My vest too. Being without it made me feel
vulnerable, like even the smallest poke of a slightly sharpened
stick would make a bloody, visceral hole in my body. Sure, my
shirt was only thin fabric but in comparison to wearing nothing it
felt like platemail.

" Can you see yet?" Blue asked from the ground, cupping her
hands over her eyes to see me. How ironic the only time I was
above her was when doing something for her.

" Not yet!" I called down before continuing my climb. Between this and the outside walls of the Red Mansion I was becoming quite the climber. Although this was much easier actually, the stones of the mansion had been slippery. This bark held firm underneath my hands. The bark felt steady and rough beneath my soft fingers as I continued up. I relished my heavy breathing by the time I reached the top, the burning of my arms, because at least I was getting away from her. Ascending into the leaves where she probably could not reach. Getting higher and higher. Pull, step, hold; don't let go. We've got five branches to go. Don't slow down. If only the tree's top would never come. An infinite oak just for me.

But. of course, as all things must, the oak ended. I had to stop for the branches grew too skinny and thin to hold my weight.

" What about now?!" Her voice was faint now, carried by the wind to some place far away. Up here she was something so quiet you could mistake her for a trick of the mind. Yes, you had just been hiking too long and started to imagine there was another color to talk to. My purple eyes took in all they could see. Treetops like a bag of dumped puzzle pieces, crowding, separating; harmoniously unharmonious. A night sky as endless as imagination, something that never faltered or ceased. Each star shined, some brightly, some dimly, but each promising of a better place. Somewhere out there apart from troubles and grief, apart from disappointment and fear, apart from me.

" Hello?!" Her wisp of a voice, more impatient now, entered my ears. Maybe if I kept climbing up into one of those weak branches I would fall and join the stars. I looked across the treetops and then down to my chest. Somewhere something was touching me absentmindedly. As if rubbing a bracelet out of nerves or a need for good luck. This foreign touch filled me with both wary and intrigue. I laid my hand over the turquoise star I could not feel, as if to let the roaming hand, the faceless stranger, know I was alright. The rubbing continued and though it frightened me, it soothed me too. I took a deep breath, took one last long look, and proceeded back to Blue.

On the ground, she asked, " Well? Which way?" I felt like saying something poetic, like 'All the ways would carry you beneath the same stars' or 'maybe the way we're supposed to go is up, towards the sky'. " East, we're not too far." She smiled and said, " Good work, Purple." I stared at her youthful face a long time and still I could not decide when so many shadows had crossed it.

Purple

My conditions were not nonsensical. I might as well tell you them, cause it's not like anyone else will bother to hear me.

Blue

I grabbed the stone under my soft hand and pulled myself up. I was close to the top of the small cliff now. My fingers clamped over the side tightly and I pulled up harshly, my arms burning.

Purple

I wanted to wait till morning, was that SO much to ask?! That was one condition. I thought walking at night was stupid; if we were under no terrorist threat then what was the rush? I certainly didn't have anything to go back to.

Blue

I brought my leg up and slid myself onto the rocks, heaving as I did. Good colors! The wilderness was so tough! But. . .I got to my feet slowly, and continued looking east. The stars sparkled over the pine treetops. I would not be deterred! I would return to the mansion, I would send a search party for my father's body, and I'd bury it! Even if I had to dig the hole myself!

Purple

She was ridiculous and mean and I was pathetic, for being bullied by a child. I was four years her age and yet I couldn't win a simple argument. Not that we were on even footing, me being her servant her whole life but still-it made me feel- ugh, I don't even want to talk about it.

Blue

I looked to Purple as he pulled himself up beside me, looking considerably less winded. I resented him for that. Stupid big arms and long legs. I rolled my blue eyes and began to walk back into the forest. Pine needles and leaves covered the ground, all looking the same in the night. Why couldn't the skytrain have crashed over a, I don't know, a pillow factory. I heard an animal hoot and I looked around warily. I waited a moment for Purple to catch up and then walked by his side. Thank Colors, I wasn't alone out here. It may be only with a stupid Purple but at least it was someone. The foliage crunched beneath us and I was thankful that he hadn't tried to leave. If he ran, I couldn't catch him and even if I did, I wouldn't be able to restrain him. He was only staying because he wanted to.

Purple

My second condition was simple as well, it was just when we found the terrorists again, I could ask them about binding before Blue killed them. I wanted to know the truth of my chest. I wanted to know how it worked. I wanted to know whose fingers I felt and I wanted. . .to know if I could do it to somebody else. .
.

Yellow

I was sitting at Red's dining table, swaying back and forth in my seat slightly. Red sat across from me at the round table. All Primary tables were round. We were all equal, anything else was disrespectful. Tradition was of high value to us. There were rules and you had to follow them. They filled me with memories of my father. A tall, sharply faced man. Always scolding me for this, screaming at me for that, I hated him somewhat. But when he died, I still cried. I probably would have cried even if he beat me like Red's mother beat him. Death, it's so tragic; almost romantically and passionately so. As if a dreary performer reading a sorrowful scene of suicide. Everyone just HAD to watch, everyone just HAD to weep.

My child and Green wandered in, formally dressed; Yellow in his cute, formal suit with buttons and that silk necktie he despised. Green in her normal green dress. Sometimes she wore white, sometimes green, I think she had a gray one but I supposed she didn't like that one as much because it was rare to see her in it. I didn't care. As long as she didn't wear Primary colors. She was a secondary. Besides that, she could wear whatever she liked.

My child sat down beside me and Green moved to sit at the back of the room with Red's Orange. Our own Orange was at home. I vaguely wondered why my child and Green had come in together.

" Daddy!" Young Red whined, " I want to eat! Where is dessert?! You promised I'd get it if I waited!" He pulled on his father's sleeve, Red smiled to him; a knowing little smirk. " It'll be right out, my child. Just-" His eyes darted to me, " wait." I smiled politely. He was planning something.

" Countdance is SO dumb!" Little Red announced and his father corrected quickly, " That's not very kind, Red. We respect the other Primary traditions, just as they respect ours." It was strange to see Red being so calm, so controlled, his voice almost tender. He used to be in his son's seat, his mother in his. I looked to my son. Yellow blinked off with boredom to the ceiling, I could tell he didn't want to be here. Probably wanted to go hide off somewhere. So unlike. . .well, me. Red's child was a spitting image of him in his youth. They looked identical, spoke identical; the same grumpy, childish impatience. Yellow was nothing like me. He was reserved, introverted, always thinking, usually quiet; as if he didn't have energy to expend on others. As if he wanted to keep all that energy in his own head for something. Not a plot or scheme, but something. I wish I knew what it was.

" Purple!" Red, older, called and his Purple's voice came back, " Coming!" His Purple was a busty, attractive little thing, I wondered if he slept with her. I mean he said he preferred men but with that little thing strutting around, how could anyone?! I smirked slightly to myself at a small fantasy. I would totally have that girl, I wonder if he'd let me sleep with her for the island. Heh, now that would be an interesting negotiation.

She wandered out, looking a bit nervous. She held a large tray of cake slices, small bowls of ice cream, cookies, cream-puffs; all yellow in color. A true countenance meal. I grinned widely, ready for those sweets. I LOVED countenance, the best Yellow tradition by far, hell it was the best Primary tradition! She sat the tray down and stepped back. I waited for her to retreat into the kitchen to get the red desserts.

" Good meal, my Primaries." she bowed and walked to the back of the room, looking uncomfortable. I watched her with confusion and then looked across the rich red table to Red. " Did your Purple. . .?" I began to ask. He reached forward and took a yellow cookie; placed it on his place. He handed a bowl of yellow ice cream to his child, who had begun to drool at the sight of the desserts.

" Did my Purple what?" he asked with a smirk. His child exclaimed, " Thank colors! I've been waiting for hours!" He grabbed his spoon and I ordered, " Don't you eat that." Young Red looked up to me with a look of confusion. " Don't." I repeated. He looked to his father with hesitation. Red held sugar dusted cookie in his hand, he waved it back and forth carelessly. Not receiving any direction from his parent, Young Red looked to me again, " B-but Yellow-" His wide, red eyes looked pouting, " I've been waiting all day." I glanced to my son, he watched this display with mild, neutral interest.

" Well, you'll have to wait a little longer. Reds eat red food, Yellows eat yellow, what you have is not red." He frowned at me, " What's the difference?" he asked with frustration, " I wanna eat!" he exclaimed, banging his small fists down.

" Go ahead." Young Red's and my head both turned to his father. Red had an elbow propped rudely on the table. He stared at me as he stated, " Go ahead, sport."

" Don't you dare!" I quickly shouted but it was too late, little Red had already engulfed the yellow dairy in his mouth.

" Unbelievable!" I exclaimed in outrage and stood up, glaring at Red, expecting an apology or at least a regretful glance! But instead, he took a bite of the yellow cookie and I was left sputtering.

" Oh my gosh!" I screamed and shoved my chair out, " You are disgusting! Horrible, horrendous! I'm going HOME!" Red shrugged and took another unrepentant bite, younger Red, a more sheepish one, and I ordered, " Yellow, get up! We're leaving!" My son slowly rose, looking to me and Red with slight confusion. Also disinterest. " Prepare the skytrain, Green!" I turned on my heel, frustration burning off me. " Yes, my Yellow." Green quickly replied and exited the room. I didn't know what Red was hoping to gain from my offence, jeez he was so disrespectful! The worst!

" Mother, I don't see why it's such a big deal." my child stated from behind me as we walked briskly down the hall. I barked in return, " Of course, you don't care about anything!" He paused and looked a little hurt; " Excuse me?" I turned on him with a snarl, " I said you don't care about anything! You have no passion, no zeal, no nothing!" I brought my hand up to the bridge of my nose, taking a deep breath, " I just know I've done something wrong with you." I looked up, opening my eyes, and his expression was painted in sadness.

" I'm sorry, Mother." He looked two seconds away from crying, " I didn't realize. . ." He looked away, " you thought I was such a disappointment."

I sighed and stepped forward to hold him, couldn't be upset with him when he looked like that. " There-there," I cooed into his ear, brushing his hair with one of my hands. " You know Mama didn't mean it." He buried his face into the cotton of my dress and held me back tightly. I smiled as I chimed, " You know I didn't mean it." but my heart felt sorrowful. I knew my words would stick with him forever; because the words my father said haunted me. " Wretched, ungrateful girl!" I was never enough for him and now I was inventing faults in my son that didn't exist. We have enough flaws without people inventing new ones for us. I gave him a minute of tending and then pulled away.

" Make sure Green has packed your things. I'll look like a pushover if I don't leave." He nodded although his eyes still looked forlorn. What? Did he want me to coddle him forever? I had corrected my mistake, he'd grown thicker skin. Thicker yellow skin, thicker Yellow pride, he'd get to the point where he couldn't cry. I had. He was SUPPOSED to be me. He would deal.

As we turned to go up to the guest floor, Green ran into the red draped hall. " My Yellow, Yellows! The skytrain's not appearing on the radar." I blinked, what? " I thought there was a glitch so I contacted Blue Castle."

" What?" I now voiced. She looked disheveled and distressed. " I spoke to Green there and he said the Blues never arrived, their Purple the same."

" That doesn't make sense." my son said quickly, eyes focused on Green. " They left hours ago." Green nodded, her green eyes showing anxiety. I quickly questioned, " The tracking beacon?" Green shook her head feverishly, " No signal. . ." We all fell into silence. " What does that mean?" my child asked after a moment. I looked to him and my eyes were serious. Ugh, fuck food color and hurt feelings and my miserable attempt at parenting. All my problems just fell out of the sky.

" It means there's been a crash." Yellow's eyes widened and I could tell he'd never considered such a thing. I looked to Green and ordered, " Get in touch with Blue castle again. Order Orange here on foot."

" Yes, my Yellow." Green replied and quickly fled down the hall. " What should I do, Mother?" my child asked and I looked at him. Oh colors. . .it could have been him. I ruffled his hair and stated, " Go tell Red to meet me in the front room." As he took a few steps, I stated, " My child, I love you." He paused and looked over his shoulder. " And I'm sorry." He frowned, nodded, and left down the hall. I stood there watching him leave, wondering if my dearest, abused friend was still alive. Wondering if I'd still have a chance to say goodbye.

Blue

The sand is gritty under my bare toes, sticking to my wet feet like they were coated in a thick layer of glue. I ran my hands through the grains with giddiness. Staring out to the water, the waves roared, I chuckled. That is probably my first memory.

Blue

" Agh! Purple!"

Purple

She was wailing at me again. Like a constant complaining tornado. " You need to hurry! It's right over this ridge!" I was exhausted. Everything hurt, I wanted to sleep for eternity. The sun's pink-yellow promising rays rose over the slope. I nodded and walked up to her sluggishly. We looked out and Blue had tears in her eyes. " Have you ever seen anything so beautiful?" she asked in awe. The glowing scarlet walls, drenched in rising sunlight, I admit, did look quite beautiful. The Red Mansion. I had seen it a hundred times before but it filled me with relief today; it was certainly preferable to dark woods and masked killers. Although I wondered what returning would hold for me. Things couldn't just continue as they always had, right? Too much had happened. Blue was dead. I was bound to this color I had never even heard of. Blue had cried in my arms, everything was very confusing. I wasn't sure how I'd deal with all of this, but however I would, I guessed it was over now.

Red

" I don't understand why you jump to the conclusion that he's dead?!" Yellow held her hands out noncombatively, " Listen, Red, I'm only telling you what the instruments say."

" Fuck the instruments!" I grabbed her shoulders violently, " We don't know THAT! STOP saying THAT!" Looking desperate and crazed for a second, she shrieked, " Maybe it's our punishment for being so cruel to him all these years!" I shoved her away harshly and she hit the wall.

" Don't say that! We'll send the Oranges! We'll find him, he's alive!"

Blue

I spotted them, walking from the east side of the mansion. Only two now, dressed in head-to-toe sable. I pointed wildly, " Purple!" He looked and his eyes filled with horror. " They're nearly there! We'll never beat them!" I screamed. The secrets I told slipped into my mind. I'd never forgive myself if someone died. Someone died because of me! I took off down the hill, running as fast as I could.

Red

" And what if he's not?!" Yellow screamed, stamping a leather boot down, " What then?!" Some yellow tears sprang to her eyes.

" He's NOT dead! You're being hysterical!"

She ran a hand through her hair, pulling it tight till it strained her scalp. " This has never happened! What will we do with no Blues!" I slapped her, " STOP TALKING! He's ALIVE!"

A knock interrupted us. We both turned to the large, richly red door, then to each other. We held a glance. . .then fought each other for the door handles.

Blue

My feet beat the ground and Purple ran beside me. My heart pounded through my skin! We wouldn't make it! The terrorists would KILL THEM!

Red

I threw the doors open and Yellow grabbed my shoulder and leaned forward to better see. I blinked widely. There were two clothed colors in front of me. One shorter and lither than the other. They wore all black, covering even the tips of their fingers and their faces; in intimidating fabric masks. Dark, ominous gauze circles for eyes.

Blue

" Wait! Red!" I screamed, " No! Shut the door!" Red and the two terrorists looked to me. I fell with a surprised, stunned shout; tripping. I would look up and Red would be dead. I grit my teeth in frustration, staring at the ground. The green grass was hit with blue tears. I couldn't stop it-I couldn't stop-. Large hands grabbed me underneath the arms and swung me up to my feet. I began to run again, and my eyes felt wet as I turned my head to Purple, who had lifted me. He stared forward with determination, his chest muscles rippling under his skin, eyes blazing. Star of turquoise out and proud like a badge of honor. I smiled slightly, then more. I could. . .I could do it. I could try, as long as he was here. We skidded to a halt.

" Red, step away from these people!" I announced strongly, blinking tears from my eyes. " They're criminals, murders, and wish you nothing but harm!" Red looked and Yellow burst past him, " Blue, darling, you're alive!" She moved not more than a foot away from the terrorists, was she not listening?! We were all in grave danger! She went to hug me and I stepped away, " This is not the time! This man killed my father!" I proclaimed, naming the most evil deed I could think of. Instead of Red slamming the door in terror and Yellow running as far away as she could get, they both froze. Red looked drenched in sorrow and Yellow like I had just cut off one of her legs.

" . . .Blue's dead?" Yellow asked and Red jumped forward onto the terrorist in front of him. He gave howl of anguish and they fell abruptly to the ground with a heavy impact! Red raised a fist up and punched the covered color in the face. The terrorist's comrade unsheathed their hidden blades and went for Red. A scream came to my throat, cut off as Purple tackled them to the ground! Pinning their arms above their head. Wow. I shook my head. Focus, Blue!

Red punched the man beneath him again and I saw the terrorist jab forward to stab him. I lunged forward and grabbed the wrist, with the blade, inches before it plunged into Red's stomach, sliding onto my knees to do so. I held it tightly and slammed the hand down. Red caught my drift and grabbed the other hand. The terrorist thrashed underneath Red, kicking out. Red punched him again with his free hand and the terrorist stilled. Yellow ran over to us with a cry of distress and I felt my heart hammering fast. We'd done it. We'd caught the terrorists.

Part Two

Blue

The Oranges came out and disarmed the terrorists properly, searching for other weapons and not finding any. They tied their arms behind their backs and I warned everyone that the last time I saw them, there was one more with them. The Oranges promised they'd be on high alert. Yellow wore this sullen, solemn look and Red this angry, hard one. I felt perhaps. . . I could have told them more gently.

We stood across from the leader of the terrorists, with him tied to a chair. What was even his plan? I found myself wondering, what did he think? He'd walk right up to Red's door and Red would just say 'Please do stab me, fine gentlemen, I wish to die'?! And he had waited so long before making a move, in fact you could argue he DIDN'T make a move, only attempted to attack in self-defense. Why? Didn't he want the Primaries dead? What was his angle?

" Does your Purple have to be here?" Red asked me grouchily, near my ear. Purple leaned up against the back wall of the dining room. I cast a glance back to him and he stared back at me with quietly sullen eyes. He wanted to stay. I owed him that much.

" He stays." I stated and Red rolled his eyes with a grumble under his breath. " Not everything's about you, Blue." he groused and I narrowed my eyes at him, " You don't know what I've been through with him, Red. He helped me get back." Red scoffed and stared at me with. . .resentment, " Oh poor little Blue, had to get her feet dirty, boo-hoo." My temper flared, why was he acting like this? Red had always been polite, if distant, from me. Where has this venom come from? " Excuse me, my father just died." I retorted with hardness.

" So did my lover, not everything is about you."

" What?! . . .You and my father were involved?" He nodded. " He was my bluebird." Something was off with the way he said the sentiment. There was nothing romantic there; no grief. It. . .made my skin crawl. I stared for a moment and then shook my head. The weird feeling, it was in my head, that's all. I tried to convince myself of that, but my instincts seemed to say otherwise; hairs on my skin stood up, goosebumps formed. I took a step away. 'Don't trust Red.' my father had said before his passing. Why would my father not want me to trust his lover? . . .It didn't make sense. Red was lying? But if he was, then why? Why now, why to me? Why after my father is dead? When he's not here to refute Red's claims.

" Well, sorry, but I think he was more important to me." I stated, crossing my arms. Abruptly, Red grabbed my arm tightly, " You're such a bitch." he growled. In shock, I pulled my arm away quickly, heart racing, sweat forming.

" Hey!" Yellow called, she had been staring at the captive, " You two can bicker all you want after this, we need to focus." Kind Miss Yellow being the logical one. " We need all the information we can get." We looked to her and Red nodded, walking forward. He grabbed the edge of the mask, tucked inside of the terrorist's heavy shirt somewhat, and pulled it off. I gasped, Yellow gave a yelp, and Red stared straight ahead. The spitting image of my father blinked softly, blue eyes becoming accustomed to the unhindered light.

Blue?

Well this could have gone better, I admit. If my broken nose and bloody face could attest to anything, it was that. I hadn't expected the Primaries to be so familiar with one another. I mean they're all ruling families so surely they knew each other but this Red and Yellow had acted like I'd slain a close friend! I hadn't even gotten a chance to explain myself. I was separated from Turquoise and they were all staring at me with quite a vast array of emotion. The stupid girl looked like she was going to weep. She took a step forward, " Dad?" she asked in the most meek, hopeful way. Ew. Did I really look that much like her father? If she asked me to read her a bedtime story, I was throwing up.

" You're alive?" Yellow asked breathlessly, gorgeous woman by the way; long, well taken care of, hair, rich, full dress, high cheekbones, tall, my type definitely, 10/10. Red said nothing, just stared with confusion, sadness, and . . .something else. Purple, bless that poor servant's soul, had taken a step away from the wall and stared at me with intense emotion. Disbelief, longing, sorrow- are you kidding me? What was this?! An episode of a soap?! This wasn't a group of ruthless, cold-blooded aristocrats, this was a mild-mannered family's mourning vigil!

" No. The Blue you knew is dead, I'm sorry." I could have pretended to be him but that would have only blown up in my face spectacularly. I wouldn't have been able to keep the charade up very long, they knew him too well.

They all stared at me like they didn't believe me. " Why?" Red asked, grabbing my shoulder; his grip pinching it was so tight. " Why are you lying?" His eyes blazed into mine. I began to sweat a bit more.

" No, seriously, I am not your Blue. I am a Blue but not y-yours." His grip tightened to a painful amount and near the end of my statement Yellow and the girl wandered up on either side of him, their visions having been obscured by him. That said, they still stood about ten feet back; scared to get too close. " But," the hot Yellow began, " there are only ever two Blues at a time. A third Blue could not exist."

" Should not." I quickly corrected, " Should not, yet here I am."

" So. . .you're not my dad?" I looked to Blue and held her beginning to look hopeless eyes.

" Yes." I replied, " Your father has passed on. I am not a ghost." She stared at me, her eyes glossing and gleaming and radiating emotion. Then she nodded. " Thanks for telling the truth," she said quietly, looking like she was about to cry, " I don't think I would have been able to handle losing him a second time." Uh, I would say 'you're welcome' but I had killed her father and attempted to kill her, so it would have been awkward, if you get what I mean.

Red looked back to the girl, " We don't know that. He could be lying, he-"

" No." Blue interrupted, we stared at her. " My dad died in my arms, he stopped breathing." She raised her arms up as if imagining the body there. " I recognize this voice from the leader of the terrorists who tried to kill me."

" What?!" Yellow exclaimed, her eyes bulging wide with concern. " Terrorists?!" Red roared with anger, sending my neck hair stick-straight! Oh Primary, I hope this was going better for Turquoise than it was for me. It would be shocking if it was going worse.

" Oh. Yes." Blue said, blinking her eyes quickly and lowering her arms, " I ran into them after me and Purple left the crash site."

" How did you escape them?!" Yellow exclaimed. Red turned and glowered down at me, anger burning off in the air around him. " You're the leader of the 'terrorist' group?"

" I can explain all of this really-" I began nervously. A red fist hit my face with a hot shot of pain and left my vision spinning. I grit my teeth for a moment, head throbbing, before having to close my lips because blood was dripping over my teeth. My nose burned and I would have whimpered if I was alone.

" Well, he's not faking being Blue." Yellow stated, watching the blue blood drip down my face. She looked to the girl, " You are absolutely sure your father's dead?"

Blue looked to her and with sullen eyes stated, " Yes, as much as I wish it wasn't true." Yellow frowned at her, " I'm so sorry, Blue." The girl nodded, " Me too. . ."

" And 'he' killed him?!" Red asked, grabbing my shirt and pulling forward. I flinched. Primaries, this was terrible. Blue looked at me and I glanced away, I didn't really want to be beaten.

" I have reason to believe he was involved, although I don't think it was ever directly confirmed by him. He did threaten my life both verbally and physically on multiple occasions though." Red glared down at me and I started, " That was only to-"

" Shut up!" Red shouted, his voice was tenor but grew deep in the middle of each word. I looked up, feeling worried. " No talking." he ordered. He pulled me up by my shirt, my rear leaving the seat but my back staying stuck because of the tight, binding rope. " This is my house. That man you killed, was my lover. That train you crashed, was my property. That girl you tried to kill, is my niece. Shut up." I did as requested.

" I say we string him up." Red said, looking over his shoulder to the other two. Yellow frowned, " We need to know how he got here before anything else."

" Through murder and assault! We know how!" Red snapped. " That's not what I meant." Yellow returned sadly. They both looked to the girl. She stared at me, me at her.

" What do you think?" Red and Yellow asked, " What do you think we should do, Blue?" Oh boy, sweat covered me, I was in quite a bit of a pickle. Colors, my face hurt. Where was Turquoise when you needed her? The girl frowned and looked behind her. " Give me a moment." she said quietly. She turned.

Purple

Blue looked over her shoulder at me, then she looked back to the terrorist leader/other Blue. I was so confused by that. There was only supposed to be two Blues, did one like spawn after Blue's father died? Is that how Primaries work? Surprisingly I knew very little about how Primaries worked. I knew that Primaries lived a long time, so did Secondaries. I knew that each Primary was a pair, a child and a parent and at some point, the parent would die. In recent memory I could only think of one Primary dying, that was Blue. Blood loss, massive internal bleeding, probably. I remember teacher commenting to me once when we were outside, trimming hedges, that a past Red, a woman Red, apparently had fallen from a third story window but lived. Crippled for the rest of her life. They say Red, her child, the parent Primary now, was so distressed by his mother's injury, he locked himself away in his room. To honor her or something, I don't know, it was all Secondary chatter. The Purple who worked here when that all happened is dead, so we have no first hand report. Other than Red, but he was still holding the bloody hostage by the shirt, did you really want to ask him? I think Primaries can only die through injury. I heard from our Green once, Secondaries were the same, but I also heard from the male Orange in the hallway that once each of your creator Primaries die, so do you. I hope that wasn't true, cause if it was, I was already halfway in the ground. Although, I was always moping about wanting to die, so maybe I should be grateful.

Blue turned and for a moment, I didn't know where she was going. Then we made eye-contact and I realized she was walking over to. . .me. Oh wow, um why? I just felt lucky she let me stay in the room. I wanted to know about binding, other than that, I didn't have a stake in this. This was a Primary matter. Yellow looked to us with depressed eyes and Red dropped the hostage, and made an angry growl. He started spitting complaints, Yellow shut her eyes, defeated, and slowly brought a hand to hold the bridge of her nose, poor miss.

" Purple." Blue said, halting in front of me. She ignored Red's noises behind her. " Yes, my Blue?" I awkwardly answered, lowering my head and height instinctively. " Thanks." she said, a smile slowly spreading over her smooth face. " Thanks?" I noticed all the little things about her then: the small wispy hairs that spread wildly around her perfectly round ears, her circle nose, shapely pronounced lips, narrow eyes, full eyebrows.

" For what?" I asked with a confused, reeling feeling. She chuckled and crossed one arm over her chest, that hand held the elbow of her other arm and she gestured with that one. " You're so silly, you've helped me this whole time. I'm thankful for that."

Helped her? With what? I suppose I lead her to the mansion but-that was it, right? She had saved me multiple times from danger, I had hardly done anything. Even when she cried, she had ordered me to hug her. I hadn't really done that willingly. The thank you didn't feel right, I was the one who should have been thanking her. But. . .I didn't want to. Even though I should have. I was so ungrateful, wasn't I? She just-she still treated me like crap, right? The only real solid she'd ever done me, that I could see, was letting me stay in this room during interrogation. For all those times she had saved me out in the forest, I would have preferred she left me. I would have preferred to die. Is that dark? Yes. Does it make me a bad color? I don't think so. I think I resented her still. She still made me feel like garbage and I didn't always feel like it, but I was better than garbage. Maybe I'm just being entitled, but I think I deserve to be treated better than that. I was not deserving of her cruel words, and maybe I had no choice but to take them, but I would not thank the color that made me feel so awful about myself. Not for a single moment. I would not respect my captor, because it was the only thing I could do against her. It was my single, cold-hearted act of rebellion. Perhaps I would be forced to serve her till Red fell, and only then I could become cold and lifeless as I desired to be. But I would not love her. I would withhold any thanks, any smile, any passing supportive glance; maybe she really needed. I would not feel mercy for the thoughtless, unempathetic one. The uncaring one. I would not love my shackles and I would not-thank her.

" Well, you're welcome." I stated passively. She nodded with a smile. She patted me on the shoulder and turned back to her people, her family. I would not be happy with the thanks, I would not be desperate for approval. No matter how much my heart wanted to hold onto the words and make them into sweet worth.

Blue?

" Are you about done?" Red snapped at the girl as she drew back to us, " Get tired of talking to the help about dusting china?!" Blue looked calmly to me, avoiding Red's scorn. Yellow placed a hand on her shoulder and Blue said, " I've made my decision." I stared to her and grinned. She had lied to me and gotten away with her life. She said she had no power compared to Yellow and Red, said they'd step all over her, but now I got it. I understood why the Primaries had stayed in power as long as they had. It's not really three kingdoms, I mean, it is, with different laws and customs and such, but they were more than allies; they were a united front. I may have blue skin but I wasn't one of them. They had years of connection and loyalty. I was a hostile stranger who killed a family member. This may be where I die honestly. . .but hey, at least I did something. I could have stayed on that mountain all my life, I could have waited for an unstable tree to smash through my roof and kill me, or-or some kind of lightning strike to do the trick, but I didn't! I gave it my best shot and I explored and schemed and loved and isn't that what life's about? Shooting straight for something and then watching in wonder as it all falls to bits. Rising, falling. Death, I am not afraid of thee.

Blue's eyes searched mine. I looked back with mellowness. " I. . .want to hear his story." Red cursed and stamped a foot, turning away. Yellow smiled and chimed, " Yes, I think that's for the best, darling." My story, huh? What a boring thing to do before I die, recite something I already lived through.

" Where should I start?" I asked with a new found tiredness, how wearisome it was to be dragged along. " Tell everything, everything important." Blue stated, she pulled a red chair out from the table and sat down. " I'm interested." I blinked at her once and surrendered with a sigh, " I'll tell you everything I know." Red leaned up against the table, arms crossed, glowering at me. Yellow hesitated a moment and then pulled out another chair.

" To start, I'm not the leader of any terrorist group. I only kept up that cover story when around my small team." I looked to Blue as I spoke and Blue explained to the others, " He had peasant colors with him." I nodded.

" Where is your team now?" Red asked with suspicious hostility. " Disposed of." I answered, Blue looked away, her eyes growing distraught. " You killed them?" Red returned in mild surprise. I nodded, " I had no need for them anymore. I wanted to take over the government, not destroy it."

Blue looked back to me, " Kill my father so you could take his place?" I nodded and added, " I knew Primaries existed in pairs, if I just showed up, I'd be a useless oddity. I needed him out of the way." Blue frowned at me, I looked to her. I had taken her father. To be honest, I hadn't ever thought about him as a color, just as a means to an end. A pawn that needed to be taken to put my bishop in just the right place. If I felt bad about it, it was probably only because I was sitting across from his daughter and about to die. I would mention that the crash was supposed to kill her too but-details, details, that wouldn't help my standing with any of these judges. Not that I had any hope of being acquitted anyway.

" If he was dead, whether you liked me or not, you would have to accept me. That or have the Blue kingdom leaderless and the Blue line die."

" What about Blue?" Yellow asked, putting a hand on the girl's shoulder.

" I didn't think a child would be a threat to the throne." I replied, looking to her, " She convinced me of that." Blue nodded and stood up, looking like she had grown sick. She walked around Yellow's chair and stood facing the back wall. I wonder what she was thinking, feeling. I wonder if I made her disgusted. Repulsed.

We sat and stood in silence. Yellow looked to me, " Where did you come from?" she asked seriously. I smiled slightly. " From a cabin in the Flame Peaks." I answered.

" The Peaks?" Red grunted, I nodded.

" Who raised you?" Yellow inquired and this was somewhere in between a police interrogation and an over-coffee chat. " My mom and dad." I answered. Red and Yellow gave me a confused glance. Blue looked over her shoulder. Red clarified, " A mom. .

.and a dad?" I nodded once more, " Yes. . ." Yellow and Red looked to each other and then back to me. Red asked with concern in his voice, " There are two other Blues we do not know about?"

" What? No. I was raised by two common colors, named Janet and Morris. They were Tan and Light Pink." Yellow looked at me with wide eyes, Blue with dubious ones, and Red grinned widely. He leaned forward and looked down on me. " You were raised by 'common colors'?! Peasants?!" His white teeth glinted at me.

" Yes. . ." I answered. " Ha!" He gave a laugh and looked to Yellow, who looked like she was thinking hard about this, " Did you hear that?" he jeered. I frowned, it's not like I had much of a choice in my situation. Yellow ignored him and asked, " How did you end up there?" I replied, " I don't know. My parents isolated me from the world and instructed me not to leave the property. I did not leave the mountaintop for a long time. Even once they past, I remained near the cabin as they requested."

" Obedient kid." Red commented, smirking. I looked to him annoyance. " . . ." I returned to make eye-contact with Yellow, " Until the day I met Turquoise, the common I brought along. I strayed too far or she wandered too close and we met. You don't want the long story but she told me of my rightful place in the world. Thus I sought to become Blue and well, that is basically all you need to know."

Yellow blinked widely and stood. " This is most troubling. I will have to check the official records." Red crossed his arms casually, seeming more relaxed than before. " Didn't we burn most of those?" Yellow sighed, " Stupidly so, yes. I'll see what I can find. The last thing we need is more stray Primaries showing up, wanting to take over." Blue turned her body completely and laid her hands on the back of Yellow's chair. " And then what will we do to him?" she asked with a tight. . .eagerness? " Wait a second!" Red exclaimed and I looked over to him, " Did you like chop wood and clean and work and stuff?"

" Excuse me?" I replied and he clarified, " At the cabin with your 'parents'." He was staring with fascinated eyes and a wide smile. " Um, yes." I answered and then flinched as he heaved over laughing. " Oh. My. Colors!" Yellow looked to him dryly.

" Yellow, what will we do to him then?" Blue repeated. This was a lot to take in, damn it. I felt like the world was swirling around me. I took a deep breath to keep the shapes from blurring.

" I don't know, Blue." Yellow answered with a tiredness, " This is all very new." The girl narrowed her eyes.

" That is not what I want to hear. You said I-" she pointed to herself, " could chose."

Yellow gave a chuckle of disbelief. " You think we should just kill him without knowing what happened?" she accused with disapproval. Red's laughter was sharp and still going. " I'm saying he killed my dad remorselessly." Blue fired back, " I've heard all I want to hear." Yellow put her hands on her hips and the two women stared each other down.

" There are questions left unanswered." Yellow challenged.

" Cold-blooded murder." Blue retorted, " I don't need answers, I need justice!"

" Wait-wait guys!" Red exclaimed, wiping an eye, " Wait!" We looked to him, both the girls' expressions showing strong annoyance. He grabbed my shoulder and I wished I could shrink away. " What did you say your parents' names were?!" I looked off to the floor uncomfortably, these two Primary women were debating whether I should have a stay of execution or not, while Red was asking me super weird questions about things I've already told him. " Janet and Morris." I answered, hoping he didn't punch me. " A-and," He shook me slightly in excitement, " what's YOUR name?" Blue and Yellow stared at me, Blue's eyes looking like they could kill. I knew Primaries just called themselves their color, I knew that. But could it hurt to answer honestly? I felt my forehead damp with sweat, my back pinch with the tightness of the ropes, it couldn't get worse, right? I was already going to die, might as well have some more things for people to remember about me. If they killed Turquoise too, there would be probably no one who would know I had existed at all. A hilltop boy with no one but the trees to talk to. I used to talk to them and name them and that was quite sad, now that I thought about it. I didn't want to be remembered only by trees, didn't want to die a nobody. Death, nevermind, . . .stay away from me.

" Bertholimule." The room hung in silence and Red gave an open-mouthed, delighted grin. " That is my name." I stated and it was final. Blue? No. I was not him. I am

Bertholimule.

Bertholimule? He'll wish he was never Bertholi-muled into this world after I'm done with him! I stalked over to him and spat on his face, which he closed his eyes and gave an expression of disgust to.

" You miserable man! You don't even feel a little bit sorry, do you?!" I screamed, " You took my father from me!" He slowly reopened his eyes and I continued, " Sitting here, pretending like you have a name, a past! Like any of that matters!"

" You wanted to hear-" he began calmly. I slapped him and somewhere behind me I knew Purple had flinched. " Well I don't anymore! I thought maybe you'd have some kind of justifiable reason for what you did. But you just wanted POWER." He glared at me and he looked like such a mess; a swelling brighter blue nose, still running blood, sweaty. Like a painter who used only used blue paint, had a breakdown halfway through a piece, and started throwing things upon a canvas; screaming.

I resented his existence. This Blue, this Bertholimule, ugh, he made my skin crawl. He blinked at me and I grabbed some of his hair and pulled it sharply, chasing a small sound of pain from his slick, blood-coated lips. " Well, do you have nothing to say for yourself?!" He glared at me hatefully.

" Oh!" Red exclaimed and I glanced at him with only my eyes, " Blue fight." He shifted weight into one hip and with a shit-eating grin, observed us. My blood ran cold. It didn't make sense. Red had said some insensitive things to me but he'd never hurt me so, why was I so on edge? So flighty. So scared. Ugh, how stupid. I glared back to the repulsive father killer.

" You are absolutely disgusting and if it was up to me, I'd string you up and let your body dangle from the rafters till it grew bloated and bloody, till the birds pecked out your eyes and tongue." His eyes grew wide in fear.

I released his hair and shoved his head away violently, then spun around, and Yellow was looking at me disapprovingly. " Are you happy now?" she asked dryly. I headed for the door, snapping my fingers, " Come, Purple." I ordered and he moved hesitantly from his place by the wall. I paused when I reached the red door frame, and placing a hand on it, looked back, my gaze; pin-sharp. " Tell me when you're ready to kill him." Then I left through the door.

When we were a good distance down the hall, I couldn't tell you where I was headed, I glanced over my shoulder to make sure Purple was there. He was. He still didn't have a shirt on, but no one had stopped long enough to ask about his star. " My Blue," he stated, keeping stride but also staying behind, " Do you think I could go check on Turquoise?" I stopped and cocked an eyebrow, " Who?"

" The peasant color that accompanied. . .the new Blue to the mansion." Purple seemed to pick the name carefully. I corrected him. " The terrorist murder?" He nodded awkwardly.

" Yes. . .the terrorist murder." he responded.

" Why would you want to check on them?" I asked. Purple suddenly stiffened and his face lost some color, " I think we should hurry, if I cannot go alone. I can feel strange things, my Blue."

" What does that even mean?" I asked, I didn't want to go see any more terrorist colors. How annoying.

" Blue!" I turned my head and saw Yellow, my Yellow. That older boy I always looked up to, the one I had desired since I was nine years old. His gorgeous full hair, tied back in a short ponytail; his buttoned, formal suit, with layers and jackets and undershirts. He was taller than me but only by a bit. I smiled widely, my soul growing warm. It felt like an eternity since I had seen him. He started quickly from down the hall and I ran to him, careless of how I'd look. I jumped into his arms and he wrapped them around me, stepping back with one foot to stable himself.

" Blue, I'm sorry about your father. I'm sorry I didn't see you when you came in, Mother sent me to my room and-"

" It's ok." I slowly lowered my feet back to the ground to hold myself. I held him tightly, " It's ok."

" I can't even imagine your ordeal." he said, I pressed my head into the yellow, stiff, pressed fabric of his jacket. " It's ok."

He pulled away, still keeping his arms laced around me. " It is though?" he asked, his yellow eyes deep in time and empathy. What a strange thing for him to ask. . . Blue tears poked out from my lower eyelids and I scoffed and muttered, " Why did you have to ask that?" raising a hand to wipe them away. " That's just unfair, I was fine." He grabbed one of my hands gently and pulled it away from my eye. " No, you weren't. You've been interrogating that guy since you got back. Did anyone ask how you were doing? If you've eaten or drank? Were YOU injured in the crash?" I shook my head no and said, " He was more important." Yellow shook his head no, his usually displeased, quiet eyes, so fierce. " Right now no one is more important than you." Some of those tears hung on the edge of falling down.

" Don't say that," I said, " I need to make sure he dies. My father is more important." He interlaced his fingers with mine and it was everything I dreamed, except full of far more melancholy grief than I had ever envisioned. Who knew all it would take for him to notice me was my father being killed in a horrible act of first degree? He looked so sad and genuine, he kissed the top of our intertwined hands.

" Blue, your father would want you taken care of first."

" Why are you being so nice to me?" My lip had begun to tremble, " I was always just annoying to you, I-I-" Yellow frowned, his thin lips turning down, " Blue-hey, listen." He brought me back close to his chest and I wished he hadn't upset me, wished I could just be left alone! I now understood why he always hid.

" Everything's different now." he said solemnly. This wasn't right, I must be dreaming, yes, everything since the crash must be a dream. I was the one who had died and I was now living in my own personal hell. Where my dad was dead and the only person left to hold onto was a stupid Purple. Where my dad's murderer was still alive, and I couldn't kill him. Where everything felt fake. Where Red scared me for some reason. Where everything was wrong and dumb and sad! I pushed Yellow away and accused, " You are only being kind to me out of pity!" He was taken off guard and raised his hands non-confrontationally. " Blue, I only-"

" No!" I shouted, " I never ever was good enough for you! You ignored me! I don't want your pathetic attempt at comfort!" He blinked widely and looked upset, " Blue, I-" I turned away, the tears spilling over and dropping down. " No! Purple, we're-" The hall was empty. . . I gave a growly shout causing Yellow to jump in surprise! I was going to get that miserable idiot so good, he would never leave my side again! I felt so hateful and angry and bitter-good! Better than fucking crying all the time! Better than the cold ocean sloshing inside each of my blue bones. Better to burn than freeze. Better to watch the water boil!

Purple

148

I didn't know where they were but I needed to find them. I had wanted to find them anyway because Blue had been so impatient she made us leave before Bertholimule could say a single word about binding. I wanted to know what had been done to me! But of course no one was going to ask questions on that. A disfigured Purple or a dead Blue? Hmm, I wonder which was more important. Please, don't kid me, a two year old could tell you that. I mean, I could have told you the answer at two years old, though admittedly, I could do a lot more than a Primary child at two years old. Kind of ironic actually, that they claim to be so much better than us, but we come out faster, larger, stronger. A Primary starts as an infant, it is supposedly because they are more intelligent so their brains need more time to develop but a Secondary comes off the press a little bigger than Young Red, ready to go. Work when we're young, work when we're old, die. Isn't life beautiful? I have no idea why Bertholimule came here, he would have been much better off in that cabin. Primaries, who I wouldn't kill for that cabin. Isolated, alone, nothing to do but make enough food to survive and even then I was free to not do that. What a miracle that would be. As I jogged, I realized I hadn't eaten in probably over twelve hours. I wondered idly if I could starve myself, honestly with how little I was noticed no one would notice until it was too late. Big jackets, I'd take up big jackets.

Anyway, the reason I had to find Turquoise was-.

" Oh heya, Purple," I turned and saw an armored woman with orange skin and orange hair. Her hair was tied up in what was supposed to be a straight looking bun, but, against her wishes, her unruly hair flopped out, and to the side, at its own choosing. " Where you off to so quickly?" Her voice was calm but high, like a shot of sugar. She was tall and muscular as all Oranges were. Taller than me in fact, but only by a few inches.

" Where is Turquoise?" I asked quickly, walking a few steps closer to her. I guessed she saw the alarm on my face for her smile decreased a bit. " Do you need her?"

" Please! Yes!" That intrusive feeling was running over my flesh, not on me, but on them. Something hot and smooth sliding across it. Made me shiver. Orange quickly began to walk and I followed, silently urging her to move faster. " Right down here," she said, " I just needed air for a minute." She pulled open a thick red door and she gasped. Frightened shock went through me. Orange, the other obviously, was on top of a woman with turquoise skin, long, thin turquoise hair, spread out along the sides of her head. She had no shirt on and he was moving his orange sex in between her exposed breasts.

" G-get off!" Orange cried and Orange looked to us in shock, " Oh, shit." he commented and I stalked over and pushed him off. He gave a 'oof' as he fell off. The woman's eyes were narrow and she was older than me. She had a look of pain on her long face, I held her shoulder to pull her off the floor. In between her average sized breasts was a patch of purple skin, just like a star. I pulled her up to a sitting position and asked quickly, " You bound me?" Turquoise blinked watery eyes. " You intervened." Oh yeah, I guess I had. . .so um. . .

" You idiot!" Orange smacked other Orange and announced. The male Orange who had assaulted Turquoise was Yellow's, I didn't know him overly well, I knew the female Orange, the one with voice like sugar, much better. I was raised and taught by teacher in the Red Mansion, she was the Reds' Orange and so we talked quite a lot, I even had a small crush on her when I was younger. Turquoise's arms were tied behind her back and she looked to be in a stunned state. " May I have my shirt back?" she asked and I looked around for it. I saw it a couple feet away, torn down the middle. Who knew that the terrorists torturing me a few hours ago would be dead, raped, or beaten in just a few more. I

151

grabbed it and laid it over her shoulder to hide her somewhat. "
I'll get you a new shirt." I said and and she asked, " Why did you
save me, Purple?" I looked to her shaken eyes with vague
discomfort. I answered honestly, " I don't know, I could feel his
dick too I guess." She seemed to be filled with remembrance, "
Ah, the binding." I nodded with sharpness and asked, " You can
tell me in a minute, can't you?" I brushed some of my hair back.
" About binding." She nodded, " It's the least I can do."

" Thanks." I replied and was distracted.

" You're such a hard-ass." I looked over and the two Oranges
were arguing. " Well, excuse me for not condoning sexual action
with criminals." Assailant Orange shrugged, " She wanted it, I
could tell." Orange hit his arm and ground her teeth in
frustration. Male Orange laughed. Turquoise whispered, " Can
we please go somewhere else?" I looked back to her and nodded.
Grabbing her shoulders, I helped her to her feet. I glanced over
my shoulder as Orange continued to scold other Orange for his
behavior. Holding the door open, Turquoise exited through it
and we left.

" Where are we going?" she asked and I said, " My room, just
follow me." We fled down the hall.

I threw open the door, the two Oranges stood bickering loudly-"
If you weren't such a prude!" he male yelled and Red's Orange
sputtered in indigence. " Hey!" I shouted, they both turned in
shock and then tripped over themselves to get to one knee.

" My Blue!" they both chanted. I glanced at the red chair they
had drug to the center of the sitting room with no windows.
There were a few, select rooms in the Red Mansion, on the first
and second floors, with no windows; in case of a storm or an
attack. The chair was empty. " Idiots, where is the prisoner?!" I
roared, stalking a few steps in the room. They looked at me, each
other, and then all around. The Yellows' Orange seemed to
panic, Red's looked quite anxious.

" W-well I-I-uh-"

" Purple." said the female Orange, she looked down to the floor
shamefully. " I believe Purple took her." I stamped a foot down
aggressively, " What use does he have for her?" Orange shook
her head no. " I'm not sure, my Blue."

" And, what?!" I continued my verbal assault, " You guys just let
him take the dangerous prisoner?!" Girl Orange looked very

ashamed, " I'm very sor-" Boy Orange stood and slid his helmet on from the nearby shelf. He slid the face mask down, " We'll find her at once, my Blue." he assured. Other Orange nodded quickly and followed her partner's example. " Yes, my Blue!"

" Good." I ordered, " Now, go." I moved from the door's path to let them go. I had wanted to chase after Purple myself, but I guess I had forgotten my place. I was a Primary, a queen; the ocean. I wandered to the prisoner's chair and added, as they reached the door, " Bring them to me here."

" Yes, my Blue." they repeated and left through the flame door frame. I smiled, sitting leisurely back in the chair, rubbing a hand along the armrest and feeling much better than previously. Making Secondaries listen to me, it was nice, reminded me of Father. Reminded me of how he said I was the ocean, how he looked at me as if I was the actual sea and he would forever be fascinated by me. . .actually I never saw that, I must have invented that. My smile turned into a frown. When Father looked at me, he loved me, but he called me on my faults as well. He saw me as a whole color, not just the admirable pieces of myself. How I longed to see that gaze just one more time, just once more. I leaned forward, crossing my arms and hunching over. Ah, and the pleased feeling fades. The water cools from its steam, my blue bones crack, and the icy water leaks, leaks, breaks. A sob takes me and I do hope- a few tears hit my knees- that those Oranges take a while.

Purple

I opened my guest room door and flicked the lights on. Nothing had changed, the bed was neatly made and the desk was clear. I hadn't slept here in a long time so it seemed like a stranger's room. Blue, senior, now um passed, didn't like to spend the night at the other Primaries' estates. I didn't care too much either way. I mean, I thought it was nice when I used to get to spend a few more hours with teacher, but other than that, not much changed. I was cooking, cleaning, and serving wherever I went, always at the Primaries' beck and call, no matter the locale. Eighteen long years.

I closed the door and Turquoise seemed a little hesitant. I jogged over to the closet and pulled out two pressed white shirts, some extras I left here at the Red Mansion, just in case I spilled wine on mine or something.

" Turn around." I requested and she took a step back, her gaze suspicious. I frowned and explained, " Your ropes." She then dubiously obeyed, saying, " Why take me all the way here to talk of binding?" The knots looked tight and bound the length of one forearm to another. I didn't even know where to begin. I bit the inside of my lip and tried to work my fingers under the coarse rope. It chafed my skin and I pulled and pulled and after a minute, I began to get them undone. When she was free, I handed her one of my shirts and she pulled it on; dropping the torn sable from before to the ground. Her breasts were exposed for a moment and when her head reemerged from the white, she scowled at me.

" Don't even think about it, boy. I've seen enough young man dick to last a lifetime." I held my hands out in protest, " I-I wasn't!" She rolled her eyes and I put my shirt on, smoothing out the fabric, much better. I coughed, cleared my throat, and said, " Look I'm sorry about what happened with Orange." She shrugged and brought her voluminous locks to the outside of the shirt. " What's happened, has happened. I only do not wish to relive it. I thank you again for your help." I would reply but she didn't stop, " But now, I need to know where Bertholimule is." I thought of the new, beaten Blue tied to a chair. There was no way I'd get the information I wanted if she knew that. " First binding, you told me you'd tell me." She nodded but did not look overly eager. " Bertholimule taught me so I'm not an expert." I nodded, " That's ok, all you know, please." She nodded, " Ok."

She ran her hands over her chest and pressed hard once she reached the center. I felt someone press my center sternum. I nodded, that was that.

" A piece of you is in me and a piece of me is in you."

" It was painful." I replied, the memories of being held to the cold forest ground coming back to me, that terrible, awful pain. She looked apathetic as she brushed some hair behind her turquoise ear. " The feeling of being flayed." I shuddered, she looked at me, I could tell my pain meant nothing to her. " The feeling of your skin being cut off and mine placed in, it is magic or at least, that is what Bertholimule told me."

" Dark magic." I commented, crossing my arms, " . . .Did it hurt for you?" Turquoise shook her head no, " That chant I was doing made the skin cells of my body want to go to you. It made my body willing to consent." I gave a frown as she finished, " It hurt you because your body rejected my cells and desperately wanted its own, as most bodies do."

" Ok." I brought a hand to my chin, " So why? Why bind me?" Turquoise shrugged, " Bertholimule made the call. We had enchanted the commons with it, claiming Bertholimule was a sorcerer with the power to make any color's color meaningless. To make us all the same. I guess we did it to show them we were serious about our whole philosophy, although we killed them right after, so. . ." Turquoise looked down to the green carpet in thought. I gave a look of confusion. " That's doesn't make a whole lot of sense." She shrugged, " I suppose, he's an impulsive boy." I took a deep breath, I had two more questions. I started with one. " So how do I become unbound?"

A pound on the door abruptly frightened us. I was tense as I heard, " Purple, come out with your hands up!" Turquoise gave me a worried glance and inquired quietly, " Have you done something wrong?" I gave an anxious look back. " I don't think so." I replied.

" I'm coming in!" Male and Female Orange threw open my door and leaped inside. Orange, male, pulled his sword out and brandished it at us. " Surrender now and unhand the prisoner!" Female Orange glared at him dryly. " Put that away. Purple is no criminal." Her partner scoffed at her, " We'll see what Blue has to say about that." Ugh.

" Blue wants to see me?" I asked and Female Orange nodded, " She wants us to bring you both down to her." I nodded and

Turquoise glowered at them and took a step back.

" Don't try to run." I said, sighing. She looked back to me, aggression flaring in her eyes. " You won't make it far."

" Personal experience?" she inquired, keeping both eyes on the armored guards. I chuckled, " Something like that."

Suddenly, I felt this violent pulling, a snap of a rubber band; quick, sharp, sting. My orientation of the room had slightly changed, I was about six feet further to the left, making me adjacent to Female Orange instead of Male. I blinked to get my bearings and as I turned my head, I was startled suddenly, a shiver running up through every part of me. I saw. . .myself. My creased, messy hair that needed a brush and wash more than anything, poking out from behind my ears and hanging around my thick neck like a starving lion's mane. Some places the animal just couldn't reach with its tongue anymore. My purple eyes, right now holding confident and challenge, my tall frame, my fresh yet rumpled shirt, my disheveled pants with small holes and tears from the crash or the falls in the forest there after. My jaw fell open as I heard myself speak, 'Myself' looked to the Oranges as they did so. " I think she'll go willingly." They looked to me and I looked down to myself. I shrieked as I saw turquoise hands and wrists along with turquoise hair laying on the outside of my white shirt. About to have a nervous breakdown, I brought one of the foreign hands up to my eyes. The fingernail was turquoise, the knuckle, even the cuticle. What the. . .

Purple

Red sat on the bed, crossing his small arms over his chest. " But Daddy says you have to do as I say!" he protested loudly. I frowned and brought my hands forward comfortingly. " Right now this is for your own safety." He scooted away from me and scowled. " No! No! No!" he shouted, eight year olds could be such a pain, " I wanna see Daddy!" I sighed and walked around the red satin covered bed, there was red lace hanging over it so I could only see the child unaverted in the middle.

" Daddy is busy."

" Daddy is NEVER too busy for ME!" We both knew that to be a lie. Red was often too busy, when he was reading new proposed laws or tax reports, when he was having one of his weekly breakdowns. His explicit instructions were usually, keep Red in his room. Of course, Little Red was slippery. He hated his room like it was an incarceration cell, maybe to him, it was.

The Primary child got everything he wanted except when he was confined there. In cases of emergency, for his safety, I could override him. He hated it, losing control for even a few minutes, it was nearly unbearable for him.

" What's even happening?! This is dumb! I want my Daddy!" I sighed and straightened my vest jacket, " Please, my Red, be patient. Your father will come get us in a minute. We just have to wait."

" I don't wanna wait!" He grabbed a pillow from behind him and threw it at me. I snatched it from the air before impact and frowned at him, then set the pillow back down on the bed. " We don't throw things."

" You're just the help!" Red spat, his cute, round face being twisted in an aggressive way, " Don't tell me what to do." I sighed heavily, feeling a tired indignance. But honestly, I was relieved for this kind of distraction, I had been so anxious before. Orange had come over to me and whispered, 'You should take Red to his bedroom.' Said something about fetching some bodies from the forest and that a kid shouldn't see the mess that was about to go down. I had asked who it was, I asked who had died, had asked if Purple was alive; he said there was no time.

He said I'd get my answers soon enough. . .

" I'm trying to keep you safe, Red. It's for your own good." I informed. Red kicked his legs in childish frustration and then flopped back, " You interrupted my dessert for this! That Yellow cake was so good! Why do the Yellows get such yummy food? It's more yummy than our food!" That was silly, the food was exactly the same, except it was dyed a different color of dye. I would know, I made it. Although he didn't need to know that now because he seemed to be finally relaxing. He grumbled under his breath but stayed laying down. I turned and busied myself with organizing some children's books and toy trucks. Then slowly-he fell asleep.

The lights were already out and the sun was rising through the window. I stared out with glum eyes, now sitting on the floor. I brought my knees up to my chest and my heart throbbed with anguish. The uncertainty was surely worse than the finality, no matter what it was. I sighed and felt my eyes gloss over. A knock at the door. I stood up quickly, looking to Red, who mumbled softly; still asleep. I crossed over the floor and asked, " Who is it?" softly through the door.

" It's Green, I'm here to update you on what's happening." I opened the door and she stood there; a pine tree in a burning field, the hall lights lit her brightly. " How is Red?" she asked formally. Her braids had pieces of hair hanging loose and her eyes were tired yet alert. Is Purple alive? The question I wanted to blurt out and yet, I knew I could not, such an emotional, dumb question. A Purple listens to others, helps in every way they can, a Purple's personal feelings . . .there is no place for them. They are useless, frivolous things compared to a Primary's brilliant judgement.

" He is well; asleep. What is the situation? I heard something about a crash." Green nodded and tucked some hair behind her ear. " The Skytrain was sabotaged." she informed and continued, " By terrorists."

" Terrorists?" I asked with fright and confusion, she made a look of contemplation, " Well, sort of."

" What does that mean?" I asked, frustration building in my chest. Is he alive? Green gave a look of surprise. " Well, there is a new Blue we didn't know about. He posed as a terrorist and I overheard some details, they used a photon diffuser to break the suction and an electronic disturber to break the safety lock. The train just dropped right out of the sky." But is he alive? "

They're, the Primaries, are interrogating him for details right now, it really is frightful that that train I've ridden more times than I could count could have just. . ." She looked down to the floor, " fell."

" And?" I grabbed her shoulders, " Were there any survivors?" She blinked at me in surprise, " Oh. Yes." Who were THEY? " The young Blue and Purple survived. Blue senior is. . .no longer with us." A tear dropped from my eye.

" Oh Primaries, Purple." Green said sympathetically and pulled me into a hug. " Don't worry, I know he's peacefully resting now." Another tear dropped and a sob of relief took me. My son was alive. He was ALIVE! I grabbed Green back tightly. " Thank you." I swore through grit teeth, " Thank you."

" For what?" she asked in confusion. " For telling me." I finished. Then holding me, she quieted. " Are you ok?" she asked, after a moment. My lip trembled and my wet eyes blinked. " Yes." I replied, " I think so. . ."

Bertholimule

" Good colors, I don't know!" I proclaimed and grit my teeth in frustration. I was covered in sweat and blood and I felt disgusting and like my back had fifty knots in it. Yellow and

Red had been grilling me for hours, or maybe only a few minutes, there was no clock in here so I couldn't tell how long it had been. " Well." Yellow said, sitting back with the black scroll and scribbling some notes down. " There's no need to shout." I frowned and Red sauntered back into the room, he had a champagne glass and a small bowl in his hands. " Mmmm," he commented and offered, " Want a glass, Yellow?" Her eyes twitched and she retorted, " We're supposed to be in the middle of an interrogation." He took a long sip of alcohol and leaned up against the chair I was tied to. " Lighten up, Yellow, we've been at this for forever. This is an Orange's job anyway." Yellow frowned and stated, " Not really." glancing down and scribbling some more notes with her quill. " An Orange wouldn't know what questions to ask, they're all brawn, no brain." Red shrugged and brought his champagne out in front of him, then back, he'd need to walk a couple feet to the table. He looked down to me and I glared at him. I was just SO glad he was feeling comfortable, at least somebody was. He brought the glass down to my lap and I wondered what he was going to do, when he shoved it between my thighs. I blushed and tightened them close together, his hand had reached far too close to my sex to be comfortable.

" Wh-what the fuck?!" I exclaimed and Red smirked, " You can hold that for me, can't you?"

" No, I can't!" I protested angrily and Yellow sighed, " Red, stop harassing the prisoner."

" I'm not!" he denied and grabbed the red spoon in his bowl and took a small bite of what look like yellow custard or ice cream. Yellow physically bristled and shouted, " Is now really the time to be provoking me with your fucking ice cream?!" He took another bite and shrugged, " There's no need to shout.";, she groaned. I looked down to the floor, embarrassed and irritated, this was so awful I could never begin to explain it in words.

Yellow sighed, exasperated, and looked back to me, " Can we go over your recruitment of the peasant colors again?" I sighed too, what a trying thing to do as your last action. " Can you kill me instead?" Red chuckled and took another bite of ice cream, " You're funny, tell another joke."

" No!" I exclaimed indigently, " I'm not your entertainment."

" Please cooperate." Yellow said with tiredness and I questioned in outrage, " You WANT me to tell a joke?!"

" No!" she spat irritatingly, " Answer the question." I groaned and Red laughed lightly.

" Ok fine, Turquoise and me scoped out lowbrow joints for a while. We specially picked colors with skills to best ensure the mission's success." Red smirked, " Spoken like a spy master." I ignored him, within the last hour or so, I was finding that to be the best strategy to deal with him. " We chose three, not wanting unnecessary people or the chance of them able to overthrow us. We chose Plasma, Dandelion, and Rosa. Plasma was an electrical engineer, Dandelion worked with large machines in a railroad company, and Rosa was a scientist who dealt with magnetics."

Yellow leaned forward with interest, " How did you get them to join you?" I exhaled and then flinched as Red grabbed his champagne by the bottom of the glass! " Would you stop that?!" I barked and he raised his eyebrows as he took a long sip. " Anyway, as I was saying," I pressed on, looking back to Yellow, " I convinced them I was a fabled sorcerer, promising equality. Many, especially Plasma, felt the color class system was unfair."

Blinking at me, Yellow asked, " The color class system?" I frowned at her, she had to be messing with me now. Next she'd ask me to recite the ABC's. Red placed his champagne in between my thighs again and I flushed.

" Well, of course you know, shade or tints of Blue, Yellow, and Red have more rights and privileges than the rest of us. The closer you are to the Primary, the more you're worth." Yellow blinked at me vacantly and Red grew a shit-eating grin. " What?" I spat at him. His eyes sparked with superiority, " You said 'us'." I blinked and realized. I blushed and silently cursed myself.

" Wait-wait-" Yellow began, " I never knew that." What? I thought, being distracted from my embarrassment. " Of course not." Red stated, crossing his arms over his chest and smiling, " You didn't need to, you have a Green to handle all the nitty-gritty."

" Wait, you knew that?" she asked and she seemed so confused, so much like she was stretching to understand. Red nodded, " Of course, I don't have a Green." He shuffled his hair pridefully. " I am the nitty-gritty." Yellow blinked and Red continued, " You and Blue shouldn't have to worry your pretty little heads about such details."

" Wait-" I interjected, " you're saying more than half our

overlords have no idea who they're ruling?!" Red chuckled, humor in his eyes as he looked to me. Yellow stood up, " I know who I'm ruling!" she exclaimed indignantly.

" Do you?!" I challenged, " How is it that I grew up on an isolated mountaintop and I know more about your land than you do?!"

" Shut it, peasant boy!" she snapped and Red laughed harder, he seemed to be the only one enjoying himself. " I'm not a peasant!" I cried in return. I was a Primary! I had blue skin!

" Well, you sure know a lot about them for being separate." she returned. I grit my teeth, " At least I do know something about them, you stupid bitch!" She made an expression of outrage and shock, then she turned her head away.

" That's it. I'm going to check the archives." She straightened her dress, rolled her scroll, and stared at me hard, before she left the room. Good, she's a bitch, I thought with pent-up aggression. Red watched her go and then stated, " She lasted longer than I thought she would." I looked up to him and was about to ask, 'What do you mean?' when he grabbed the champagne glass from in between my legs. He threw it fast and hard to the floor and it shattered; red alcohol exploding everywhere! My jaw dropped open in shock and suddenly Red had maneuvered in front of me. A large hand jutted in between my thighs and I gave a cry of surprise as it groped me. I looked up to Red and his blood eyes glinted. " Are you ready to get wrecked, peasant boy?" Oh Primaries, what was happening? He touched me violently and inappropriately and I struggled and whined. Flush stained my face. No. No. No! This couldn't happen! He slipped his hand in my pants and past my underwear, " Colors," he breathed out, breathing heavy, leaning in so he was practically overtop of me, " Colors, you're packing." I screamed in hopes of help or just because I couldn't think of anything else to do. Beaten, interrogated, raped, killed. I saw my story so well. The trees would be the only ones to wonder what had become of me, the lonely but cheerful boy, Bertholimule, who spoke to them. I didn't actually think I was destined to be a king, nor that I was a God as those common colors thought, but I was more than that somehow. I was Bertholimule and I had inherent worth, when I chopped wood with Dad and tended to the foul with Mother, it wasn't all for nothing. . .I mattered, I mattered! And I wouldn't let him get away with this. My arms were bound and my face sore but I still had my mouth.

" Llion meta roto elka mons caso eno toco amon-" Red froze and

170

then convulsed, his hands grabbed onto me in shock and then he pulled away, stumbling a bit. His eyes were wide with fear and confusion.

" Wha-ah!" He gripped his chest, his fancy red coat creasing under his hands. He trembled slightly, " What are you-ah?!"

A tear pricked my eye and I stared hard and chanted as loudly and quickly as I could, " Moto lela kiki ono adda-"

" How do you-ugh?!" He stumbled further back and pressed his hands over his chest, eyes growing in panic. I'd bind him and take his place! Then we'd see him try to touch anyone! Through my black layered shirt a blue glow emerged and I felt overwhelmed, that wasn't supposed to happen. That had never happened before but in a frozen, blind panic the chant continued.

" St-stop! Pl-please!" Red pleaded and a strong red glow started to emerge from his jacket.

" Alki omca ina inca momoli sha!" He gave a shout of pain as a small red ball of something moving, liquid floating, broke from his chest, tearing the fabric of his jacket with the burst of a button. " Menen akar alsas monto-" The chant slowed but still continued, sweat dripped down my brow, heart hammering away in my chest. Suddenly, I felt something passively come through the skin of my chest and I looked down, eyes wide, to see a floating ball, similar to the one from Red's chest. The chant from my mouth slowed and then stopped. Red was breathing heavy, still holding his hand over his chest, standing on shaking legs. I was breathing heavy too and we made, on both parts frightened, eye contact. Then his focus shifted and mine did as well. The two floating balls of liquid orbited each other unsurely in the middle of the space between us. One red and one blue; endlessly turning.

~~Purple~~ Turquoise

We walked down the hallway and I was between both the Oranges. They were smaller than the folk tales had lead me to believe, still large but not quite giant size. They certainly had the personality of brutish giants though, I stared hatefully at the Male Orange. I would say I still felt violated but that wasn't exactly true, see I was feeling electricity; foreign, all over. The way I always did when I inhabited a body that was not my own. I looked over to Purple in my body and he struggled, Orange holding his re-tied arms.

" Son of a bitch!" he spat in my voice which sounded higher than

I like to think it did, " I said I'm not Turquoise!" Orange rolled his eyes and growled, " And I'm Yellow. Now shut up." He shoved the trapped color forward and Purple nearly tripped over his own feet, my own feet? Ugh, whatever. " But I'm Purple!" he exclaimed desperately and Female Orange gave me a confused look. " What is she talking about?" she whispered to me. I shrugged, " I don't know, probably just scared, saying whatever she can think of." Orange frowned, sympathetically I think, and Purple gave a protest of frustration, struggling again. I can't say I didn't feel a little bad about doing this to him, but I couldn't risk execution. Bertholimule was going to live as a magnificent and honored Blue within these gorgeous walls, just how we planned, and they'd never let a common stay. The plan was always for me to become a Purple, I had nothing against Purple; it was nothing personal. We were greeted aggressively at first but once they realized Bertholimule was a Blue, they'd accept him and as a Purple, they'd accept me too.

Orange held open the door and I followed a squirming Purple, escorted by Male Orange, through the door. I only had to remain calm, appear confident, and I could fool them. Me and Bertholimule had watched the Primaries for some time now and Purples were submissive, quiet servants who the Primaries paid little attention to, how hard could it be? I would deceive them,

I'd be a Purple, and then me and Bertholimule would rule together at last.

Turquoise Purple

I was so unbelievably screwed! Beyond screwed! I was fucked! So fucking fucked! As soon as I locked eye contact with that little bitch, I knew it. I was a dead man. Blue was forever merciless. Her eyes quickly found 'Purple's' to my slight surprise. "You fucking idiot!" she exclaimed and stalked forward, Turquoise clearly shocked as Blue grabbed her shirt and pulled 'me' forward. I felt my forehead dampen and thought, hey. . .well, at least some good can come of out of this. Blue stared forget daggers, try blood-dripping claymores at her and Turquoise gave a look of surprise and panic. She flashed me a panicky glance and I smirked, couldn't help it, stealing MY Primary-damn life? Her punishment would be seeing just how unbelievably shitty it was.

"I didn't give you permission to leave me, you frickin' imbecile!" Female Orange flinched and looked to Turquoise sympathetically, she really was nice; Turquoise blurted, "I-I'm very sorry, my Blue!" Blue grit her teeth and growled, "You will be." A small, disbelieving laugh left me. Thank Primaries that wasn't me, thank fucking Primaries. Blue's eyes didn't so much as turn to me! How lovely it was to be invisible!

" I really am sorry!" Turquoise repeated and my voice sounded needy when it was pleading. I cringed, ew. Did I always sound that pathetic? Gross. I'm blocking that from my mind. Suppressing forever. Deep down.

Blue shoved 'Purple' back and Turquoise stumbled before catching herself. " What was even SO important?!" Blue demanded, Turquoise gave me another worried glance. I shrugged, smiling. Why would I help her? She took my body and anyway, helping people got you nowhere.

" I-I sensed something weird because of the bonding between me and the common, my Blue." Blue cocked a full eyebrow skeptically and then looked to me. " And-" she prompted, looking back to Turquoise. " Was it anything?" Turquoise sweated and stuttered, " W-well u-um." You better come up with a good lie, I thought, Blue's a loose cannon. If you tell her the truth there's no way you'll possibly be able to gauge how she'll react.

" O-Orange," Turquoise nervously pointed to Male Orange, who was holding my arms tightly behind my back, " w-was assaulting her." Blue blinked widely between the two of them and then to me with this awkward, confused expression. I shrugged.

" O. . .k?" Blue answered and I wondered how much of that she understood, " That's no excuse for leaving me." she finished and I sighed, glad to see the selfish brat never changed.

" What?" Turquoise asked in quiet disbelief, " My Blue, she was being raped."

Male Orange, behind me, interjected, " Just sexually assaulted, my Blue, Purple exaggerates. I would never contribute to more peasant trash." Turquoise gave a look of outrage to him and I wore a dry expression. Everyone in this Primary-blessed mansion was a fucking horrible color, weren't they?

" U. . .h." Blue looked between the two of them, cleared her throat, and then repeated to 'Purple'. " D-doesn't matter. What do you care about 'her'?" She gestured to me with disgust. I nodded in agreement, both myself and Turquoise were pretty disgusting.

" S-she was a-assaulted, my Blue! How could you allow that?!" Blue looked flustered, " S-shut up, it's not like he's mine!" She made a pouting expression as she pointed to Male Orange and then crossed her arms. " If Yellow wants the behavior to stop, she'll do something about it. It's not my business what he does with the lackey of the disgusting color who killed my father!" Female Orange looked extremely uncomfortable watching this. Turquoise looked outrage, 'my' face curling in indignance.

" You'd condone rape?!" she exclaimed and Blue flopped some hair over her shoulder, clearly irritated.

" Don't mind her, Purple." I stated to Turquoise, who was wearing my skin like a suit, " She probably doesn't even understand what that means." Blue and Turquoise's gazes both looked to me and then, Male Orange hit me harshly over the head, causing me to flinch. 'Ow' I mouthed and Orange tightened his grip on my arms, pinching the skin of my back.

" Shut it, peasant! No one asked you to speak!" he barked. I frowned and looked down to the floor, my head stinging softly. Man, I couldn't catch a break no matter who I was. The more I experience, the less I want to. Blue walked a step in front of me and grabbed my chin, holding it with painful pressure. " I'm sorry, who are you, peasant?" I frowned and answered, " Turquoise." Turquoise looked to me with surprise. I met her eyes and she seemed to ask me why I was just going along with this.

My answer for her was easy, what was the point? What did I have as Purple that I didn't have as Turquoise? Maybe they'd let me go, let Turquoise go, I could return to a peasant village and I'd be poor but I'd be free. Purple could never be free. Maybe this was fate, maybe a stroke of good fortune.

" Well, 'Turquoise', shut your mouth." Blue began severely, " I'm Blue and I'm a Primary and this is my castle." She stared at me harshly and finished, " And that is my. . .Purple." I blinked widely at her as her expression slowly shifted, her eyes changed from cold anger to a cautious curiosity. She moved my face back and forth and ran a thumb down my skin. Her thumb was cold. The Oranges looked to each other in uncomfortable wary and Blue asked 'Purple' without looking away from me, " Why does this color look so. . ." She leaned closer in until her face was all I could see. Her eyes widened and she drew back, " Purple?" she asked. My eyes widened and my bottom lip dropped open just a bit. No. What?

Turquoise

That was impossible.

Blue

I looked between the two of them and the one who looked like Purple said, " M-my Blue, what are you talking about?" They certainly sounded like Purple, but now that my anger had faded, it didn't. . .look like him. I mean they did but, the eyes, I looked back to Torquise's. Yes, those eyes. Dead, quietly sad, they sparked to life in anger and I don't think I'd ever seen them happy, Purple happy. They were sad eyes, they were my Purple's eyes and though the iris and pupils were wrong, I was confident in that. I knew Purple and I knew Purple's eyes. " Purple?" I looked to the imposter. " Yes, my Blue?" they responded.

" What did you do in the forest to locate the Red Mansion?" 'Purple' frowned and then slowly said, " I followed you, my Blue."

Purple

Damn, she messed up. I felt mild disappointment, well, maybe a Purple would be better than being a peasant. I didn't exactly know otherwise.

Turquoise

Blue stared at me sharply and raised a hand, " Orange, restrain him." Female Orange hesitated a single moment and that was all the time it took for me to decide to dart for the door. I just needed to tell Bertholimule. I needed to tell him I had failed, stupidly failed! How was I supposed to know that Blue was so close to Purple?! Maybe I should have guessed after she bargained for his life. . .but still! I ran underneath the doorframe and I heard Blue exclaim, " Get him!" behind me. Now that my eyes weren't obscured by my black, gauzy mask, it shocked me exactly how red this place was; red ceilings, red floors, red vases, red portraits of current Red, his son, and my guess was, past Reds. Although now was hardly the time for such observations. What were we going to do?! How could she even tell us apart?! Me and Purple looked exactly the same, sounded exactly the same, I effectively WAS Purple right now! The fact that she could tell was ludicrous, unbelievable! I felt a shot of pain through my left leg as I sprinted down the hall, Purple had an injured leg, in fact a good majority of this body dully ached. Just great, this day just couldn't get any better. It couldn't! Damn.

. .

I turned a corner and realized I should have demanded Purple give me that information on Bertholimule's location before I revealed my true objective, true blown objective. I heard footsteps behind me and I looked over my shoulder, not slowing my stride. " Halt Purple!" Female Orange demanded, running frighteningly fast on her long, thick legs. Primaries, she had to be eight feet! I turned my head back and I knew I wasn't going to be able to outpace her. Her breathable armor clanked softly as she ran, contrasting the loud, brash sound of her heavy feet. I grabbed a red stand, with a red bowl of rubies atop, and slammed it down behind me. Orange vaulted it and I paled, jeez! My heart pounded as I skidded into the next hall, a woman with green skin, green hair, and no time to explain the rest, greeted, " Oh, Purple, it's good to-" I hit her shoulder and she gave a cry of surprise as her tray of drinks fell. The liquids splashed into the carpet. I spotted a door and opened it, slamming it closed not a second before Orange pounded on it. " I'm not going to hurt you!" she promised and I locked the door as she pulled on it. " What did you do, Purple?!" I was breathing heavily and in an adrenaline-full panic, I saw a bookshelf to the left of the door. I sprinted to the left side of it and tried to push it. It was heavy and every muscle in my arms strained. Grunting, I moved it into place in front of the door. Panting, I placed my hands on my knees and leaned over.

" Purple!" Orange cried and sweat dripped down my forehead, my chest expanded out and collapsed inward. I'm pretty sure I was gonna throw up.

Purple

" So, what happened?" Blue asked, taking a few steps back and sitting back in the red wooden chair. " You can release her." she said offhandedly to Yellow's Orange. He stepped away and looked to the Primary unsurely. " You can also go help Orange capture Purple." He looked between the two of us and slowly nodded. Hesitantly, he made his way to the door and left. We were left in the silence. The room was on the smaller side of the average, for the Red Mansion, and had no windows. It had a small, red, wooden table in the corner, with a latched chest nearby of the same shade. I sighed and sat down on the floor, sitting with crossed legs.

" It's a long story." She frowned and kicked her legs so they hung over the chair's armrest. " Do begin then." I nodded and cleared my throat, beginning to fear making her upset, now that I didn't have a different identity to hide behind. " Well it is as Turquoise said, I felt her being assaulted and I intervened." Blue stared at me with listening, neutral eyes. " Then I took her back to my room to give her a shirt, Orange had torn her old one." Blue made a face of disgust, " Why would he do that?" I shrugged and replied, " Um, he probably wanted to see her-" I refused to finish that statement. She turned forward, dropping her feet flat back to the floor. She looked away and looked behind each of her shoulders, as if fearful of an eavesdropper.

" Is it wrong that makes me really uncomfortable?" She shivered and I slowly shook my head no. " That's normal for most colors I think. Assault is considered wrong by most people." She looked at me and asked, with wide, concerned eyes, " Do Secondaries do that a lot?"

" Uh," I looked away uncomfortably, " not more than anybody else. . ." She looked to be thinking and placed a hand on her chin. " How do you like. . .tell that?"

" What?" I responded and she shook her head, " Never mind, a talk for a different time. Why are you currently in a peasant body?" Some sweat found my face, oh yeah, that. " Well, when I got Turquoise a shirt, the Oranges started pounding on my door." Blue nodded and added, " I sent them after you." I gave a dry countenance. " Thanks, got that." She shrugged. " Then," I added dramatically, " in a flash, I was in her body and she was in mine." Blue cocked an eyebrow, " That doesn't make a lot of sense." I shrugged, " I guess not. . ."

Rubbing her pointed blue chin, she inquired, " Do you think it had something to do with the binding?" I nodded, my eyes serious, I didn't know all of its secrets just yet. " Do you think it can be reversed?" she asked and I nodded unsurely, " Um, I don't have any reason to believe it can't be." She nodded, " Good. It'd be weird to have you be a girl forever."

I frowned and asked, " Wait, wouldn't you throw me out if I wasn't Purple? You know," My face was soaked in a forlorn matter-a-factness, " -if I can't be changed back?" She looked to me in surprise, " Why would I?" She asked it as if I had just told her fish flew and birds swam. But I hadn't said anything nearly so ridiculous. " You know, because then I'd be Turquoise; a peasant. I wouldn't be Purple."

She leaned back and fixed her long hair. " So?" With confused eyes, I watched her in her chair. She gave a small smile. " I'm a Primary, I make the rules. If I want you-I want you. You aren't yesterday's garbage to be thrown away and never thought about again." Her smile faded to a more serious expression, " You mean something, Purple. You mean something to me." I physically leaned back and looked around in surprise; as if looking for a witness, to confirm I was really hearing this.

" Excuse me?" I asked and she stood up, " You heard what I said. I meant it too, so you better not pretend to be anybody else again. You are to tell me about everything that happens to you."

After a moment, " E-everything?" I questioned and she nodded.
" Um. . .my Blue," I rubbed behind my neck, inquiring, " doesn't
that seem a bit. . .excessive?"

" No." she stated and we fell to silence, her staring into my eyes
with this cold calmness, surged with control and power.
Something unchanging but damaging. Stable but uncomfortable.
Like an ocean frozen solid, me hopelessly sliding across the ice.
. .I had to look away with worry in my bones.

Yellow

I wandered into the bar area of the billiard room. It was lit with
small, hanging red lanterns and was a long room like a rectangle.
I saw the back of. . ." My child?" He turned as I walked up, my
short heels clicking across the red tile floor. " Oh, Mother, hi."
He sat on one of the plush red bar stools with aging, adorned
legs. Red was all about flare, flare and establishing power over
people. From what he did to Blue to yellow pudding, it was all
about the flaunt of what he could get away with, the boast of his
strength, the boast of himself.

I came and sat beside my child, he looked somewhat disheveled;
neck tie loosened and long hair breaking free from his thick

ponytail. He raised up a yellow wine glass, full of yellowish liquid that still had the tannish glint of champagne. He took a long sip and I asked, " My child, what are you doing here?" He smiled at me weakly and answered, " What does it look like?" before taking another sip. I frowned and tapped my hand on the counter, which was made of granite, painted in a glossy red. You could still see the natural swirls and shapes of the stone come up through the artificial color.

I could hardly condone such a thing as emotionally drinking but I didn't feel it would be right to lecture because, I was here to do the same thing.

" Where's Green?" I asked and he answered, " Getting me more drinks." I nodded and we fell into silence. " Were you really that shaken by Blue's death?" I asked with sympathy. He shook his head 'no'. " But by a new Blue, and the world turning upside down, yes."

" Drinking is not the answer." I replied because I knew I should. " Neither is dancing." he retorted and took another sip. " People aren't going to stop their waltzing." I chuckled lightly, " True, I suppose. . ." I rang the red bell and hoped Green hurried. I needed something to take the edge off this throbbing headache.

The chime of the bell and the sound of the wine glass being placed down on the counter blended for a moment. I looked over and my son looked as ragged as I felt. A sigh left me, maybe we were more similar than I liked to believe. After all, as a child I did remember I enjoyed being alone too, not to my child's obsession but I could take in the silence. Nothing but your own breathing and footsteps. I would hop over ragged stones, the waves roaring against them. I opened my eyes, when had that been? Yellow took another sip of champagne.

" Mother," he began, looking upset, " you don't really think there's something wrong with me. . right?" I looked to him and straightened up, " Are we still on this, Yellow? I told you, I didn't mean it." He frowned and his eyes clouded in anger, " But you did. . .didn't you?" I watched him dubiously as he lifted and finished his glass. His Adam's Apple bobbing as he swallowed. " I didn't." I insisted calmly.

" You're such a liar." he retorted darkly and slammed the glass down. I inhaled and felt a spike of anger, " Well, maybe I do! Is that what you want to hear?!" I questioned, turning to him fiercely. He gave a harsh gaze and then it softened sadly, " . . .No." I 'tch'ed and spun back to the counter, I rang the bell more ferociously this time.

" Mother. . ."

" What is it?" I spat and Yellow, with a frown, asked, " Do you think I'm a bad person?" Ugh, I didn't have time for his teenage angst. " What does it matter?" I asked him, he looked down to his empty glass, " It won't change your opinion of yourself either way. People believe what they believe. Each color determines their own morality and worth inside their own head."

" Why isn't everyone super good and moral then?" he returned and I wondered how many drinks he had had.

" Because most colors are bad." I answered and he looked to me with careful yet drunken thought. " Then why do most colors choose to be bad? Wouldn't most people choose to be good if given the chance?" I smirked and brushed my hair behind my ears.

" You'd be surprised." I replied, I mean I should know. I'd chosen to be bad most of my life, that or neutral, to be good, to be truly good, that was something I never had the patience for. Being good meant sacrificing your own desires because the majority of people would suffer because of it. Putting the good of others, above the ambitions of yourself.

" I tried to comfort Blue." he revealed and I was pulled from my thoughts. He pushed some hair from his face. " She basically told me to get lost." His eyes shimmered with sadness and I prompted, " So?" insensitively. Snatching the bell, I violently jangled it. Where was that stupid Green? He looked to me hazily and stuttered, " S-so? She hates me!" I rolled my eyes, " I could only imagine why she might be irritable right now." He frowned at me and then sighed, ". . .Why'd he have to die, Mother?"

My soul felt heavy at the mention of Blue. I gave a dark chuckle. " Because a good person always had to die for a bad color's sins." Yellow looked to me and smiled as if I had said something thoughtful. " Ah." he said and put an elbow on the cold granite. He leaned his face into his palm and his yellow cheek smushed against his it. He smiled and said, " So that's why colors chose to be bad, the bad ones survive." Guiltily, I nodded.

" Someone has to." I answered solemnly, he nodded. I looked away and felt my eyes begin to water, my vision blurred slightly with the wetness. The bell lost its distinction from the granite and everything blurred into a screaming red.

" Alright," Red said, slowly, carefully, as if I was the general of an opposing army, " alright, I'm going to go forward and reabsorb my depon." Depon? " Ok?" I was still breathing heavily and felt suddenly very tired. If I let him reabsorb-my eyes glued onto the red blob, perfectly swirling in a sphere-that, the depon or whatever it was, how did I know he wouldn't attack me again? I looked to him and he waited for me to give a reaction. The large, blood man looked suddenly very serious. I couldn't ask what the blob was, that would give away my advantage, and I needed every one I could get. " And if I did-" I started, using my best powerful adversary voice, which made my voice grow lower, 'Your head, Blue.'. " -then what would you do after?"

He scowled and if I wasn't mistaken, his cheeks flushed, " I'll leave, I really will."

I cocked an eyebrow and questioned confidently, " Leaving me tied to a chair? You'd come back and smash my head in." He frowned but didn't deny my accusation. " You better untie me first." He gave a legitimate growl at this and through gritted teeth added, " After I absorb my depon back." He took a step forward.

" I'll begin to chant again." I threatened, narrowing my eyes. I actually liked to play such dramatic games. Becoming steely, confident, in complete control. I often played pretend by myself back at the cabin; the trees becoming the villains or heroes, or sometimes victims; for me to slaughter or save. Performance came natural to me like another skin.

Red fisted his hands and his irises seemed to shake. His eyes burned into mine. " Don't you dare. I'll strangle it." he threatened.

Tossing hair out of my face confidently, I smirked and mentally took note of it. " Then it'll save both of us some effort to untie me, Scarlet." He bristled at the nickname and I winked. Well at least I had guts going for me, although I had a feeling if I wasn't careful, those guts would end up all over the walls.

" Watch your tongue!" Red snapped and I let my slight smirk drop to something more severe. " Watch your step." I retorted, " I'm not afraid to finish this." I gestured my head to the spheres of almost paint. Red looked between me and them with horror and yelled, " Why would you ever WANT that?!" He was becoming hysterical, I had to calm him down, I needed him to use his reason. Hysterical people did things that didn't make sense, did things purely based on emotions, regardless of the logical consequences. I needed logical consequences, I needed him to untie me.

" I don't, but I also don't have anything else to lose, Red."

" Bull!" he retorted, " They always can take something else away, you are only free in death! Do it! I'll kill it and then we'll see how much you have to lose!" His eyes flared and a sick smile took his face, " I bet you've never seen somebody die, Bertholimule."

" I've killed people." I replied coolly.

" So have I!" Red exclaimed, pointing to his chest, " Hundreds of people! It would take a river to hold all their rainbow blood!" A drop of sweat descended from my clammy skin. " And I have no qualms to kill another." he finished. Then he gestured his hands out and asked, " Have you ever seen a child die, Bertholimule?" I tensed and hardened my gaze, I had not. Was the 'it' he had spoke of a child?

" Well, come on!" he called tauntingly, " Let's make today your first!" I had lost my advantage. Red waited as I stayed silent.

Then he smirked as he confidently proceeded to his depon. He would rape me if I didn't do something, now he wasn't just lustful, he was angered. It would haunt me forever. As he grew close, the red ball shifted out of its orbit with my depon and neared him. With a motion of his hand, it soaked through his fabrics and entered back inside of him. He stared at me and grinned. My blue depon now began to move in a more aimless circle at about Red's waist level.

" If you don't leave," I threatened, " I'll rip your depon out again." His smile dropped and he paused. " You are . . .determined." he stated finally. I dryly replied, " Well, we just met. I think you should at least take me to dinner first." He cracked a grin and shook his head as if he couldn't believe me. " You ARE funny." I stared at him and he nodded, " Ok. I'll leave. Good luck being completely immobile with an open depon." He flicked the blue ball and it shuddered, moving away from his hand. I couldn't feel it. What even was it?

True to his word, he crossed over the tile floor and left through the tall wooden doors. I, left in the dining room alone, cried a single tear. Then tears of frustration I'd been holding back since I got to this stupid place dropped down my face. My face, that still throbbed with pain and wore a coat of dry blood, was wetted. I would lie on the ground and sob there, but I was still tied, still stuck, so I sobbed with not even my own hands to dry my eyes.

Orange

I jogged down the hall and felt a little worried about that peasant and Primary. If the peasant was somehow a friend or even a favored acquaintance, which I had never heard of before but hey, first time for everything I guess, of Young Blue I was certainly fucked. I sure hope they weren't, I didn't want to get in trouble. Orange complained I had a 'sex addiction', I personally argued that it was a difference of the sexes, of course a woman wouldn't understand. A man's sex drive was all consuming, I probably thought about sex more than, hmm let's see, anything. I fucking needed it. That hot, busty peasant all alone with me, I didn't really want to but I just couldn't resist. I'd fucked so many people, at least compared to my fellow Secondary males, which I must fairly emphasize there weren't many of.

There was Blue's Green and that kid of a Purple. I'd fucked Green, female of course, we hooked up every once and awhile, I fucked Orange, she may be bitchy but she was a size where she could actually keep up with me. She would complain about it but I knew she enjoyed it. I even fucked Red's Purple once, she had seemed so unsure of herself, it was cute. Sometimes I walked along the manor's roof and imagined the towns of peasant women of all shapes and sizes, all just begging to be taken. You might ask, 'Shouldn't you be on look-out instead? Aren't you a guard?' or maybe, 'What the hell is wrong with you?'. There is an answer to the first one. Also if you asked the second one, you're probably a girl. Anyway, I'm an Orange. I'm the guard of my Primaries and all their possessions. How heroic, how dutiful-how boring. If you didn't take into account recent events, Yellow's never been under attack in her whole life, the same goes for her son-of-a-bitch son. Wait, that's not true, once a squirrel came inside through an open window and spooked her. I spent five hours trying to coax it out from a vent with squares of cheese, some royal protector I was! As far as I was concerned, an Orange's job was to walk the grounds aimlessly and lock every window, door, and vent when the Primaries went to sleep. To wear fancy armor and carry an impressive sword. I could always tell when Yellow wanted to intimidate Red, for she brought me along on their frequent visitations. I'd just stand uselessly at the back of the room, back straight and metal gleaming. Those trips annoyed me. I loved being left alone at home. So much, heh, privacy.

Sorry, what was I talking about? Oh yeah, the point was I had no purpose and. . .I think I was also talking about sex, but then

again when wasn't I? I heard Orange's voice down the hall. "
Purple!" I sped up a bit and then slowed when I turned the
corner. Green was staring over at my fellow Orange, slamming
her fists onto a door to one of the studies. We were in the eastern
most hall of the second floor. I jogged over and me and Green
made brief, eye-contact, her eyes concerned as I passed her.

" What's the sitch?" I asked and Orange turned, halting her
pounding, and stated, " Purple locked himself in here, he won't
open the door."

" Did you try picking the lock?" I asked and then her eyes
widened and she flushed. She unzipped the small bag on the
outside of her white, orange-edged armor. She pulled out a red
key and smiled sheepishly. " Master key. . ."

" Oh. . ." Orange shoved it into the lock and Green asked, "
Orange, what's going on?"

" Nothing, babe, but you ought to step back, this could be
dangerous." I replied. She frowned and stepped away. Orange
swung open the door and behind it was thick, shiny, polished red
wood, covering the entire doorway; blocking our way. " What

the heck?" I asked aloud and Orange traced over it with her gloved hands, " It's a bookshelf." she analyzed.

" He barricaded the door?" Orange nodded to me, her visor glinting in the hall light. I placed my hands beside hers and announced, " On three. One, two," We pushed forward, pushing with the height and weight of our large bodies. " Three!" The bookshelf budged and then slowly began to tip forward. With a smash on the floor, me and Orange entered in, crawling over the shelf. Ya know all this capturing and prisoner watching and problem solving kind of did it for me. It made me feel . . .alive. Like I was born for this. Certainly beat being a squirrel catcher. We looked around and he was standing right near the door. I turned and he slipped out the door, slippery fish.

" This way!" I called and catapulted myself back out the frame. Green was hiding behind a side table with red roses atop. " He went that way." She pointed down the hall. I nodded and me and Orange took off down the hall.

" Where's Turquoise?" Orange asked, not even close to winded. " With Blue." I answered, " Isn't that dangerous ?" she returned. I shrugged, " Guess so, she told me to follow you." We turned the corner, " A Primary wouldn't say it was ok if she felt unsafe."

" But she's just a child." Orange answered, " We've already lost one Blue, I don't want to lose another." I ignored her, trying not to doubt my decision, and increased my running speed down the long hall. The bastard disappeared down the end of the hall and I knew he had begun to descend the staircase. There was no way we could cut him off. There was only three staircases that linked the Red Mansion's floors. One at the far west of the house, the far east, and one in the center. We were already too close to the east. For being smaller than us, Purple was quick, I'll give him that, but he didn't have the stamina we had. We'd catch him, catch him if we had to run across the entire Red empire.

Our feet pounded down the steps, skipping multiple at a time. When we reached the bottom, there was no sign of him. With a growl, we began to check the rooms.

Turquoise

I entered a large room with a glittering red chandelier, a long, polished dance floor, a red piano; the room as wide and long as probably any building I'd ever been inside. The ceiling was domed, portraits of Reds on the inside. It reminded me of the Red basilica my grade school class had taken a field trip too when I was just a little girl. Unfortunately, I didn't have time to stay and admire the fine mosaic work.

I spotted an open doorway on the opposite side of the room. I ran over to it and I whipped through. Breathless, I froze. There was a large parlor area, that at one end, had the front doors me and Bertholimule had originally been drug through. There was a long, oval rug, of what looked to be the softest material in the world, on the floor; it has a complex design of mountain lions on its surface. There was a circle of stands with decorations on them; china, jewels, candles, vases. The room opened up and to the left there was a long hall. There was a marble staircase leading up, to my side. But all of that seemed unimportant compared to the man sitting in front of two closed red doors. He had his legs crossed and leaned back like he owned this place. He had stiff, slicked back hair that broke off in places and hid small bits of his forehead. He had aloof yet alert eyes, like a house cat, and wore pressed dress pants and a proper, wool jacket. One strange thing I noticed right away was the hole directly in the middle of his chest, his jacket fabric, and it looked like his undershirt and vest as well, were torn. Right where a binding would take place, did Bertholimule try and bind him? Was he unsuccessful? I didn't see any blue skin. Why would he have to resort to that? I began to grow anxious.

His eyes turned to me. " My, servant boy, you seem out of breath, running to do some last minute laundry?" He smirked at me and flopped some of his free locks out of his eyes. His hair fell to the bottom of his neck. I was silent, mind racing, chest contracting quickly as he frowned.

" Cat got your tongue? Oh well. . ." He looked away and shifted forward, straightening his jacket tails, which tucked around his hips. He looked back to me, " I wanted to have a chat with you anyway." My mind was panicking, Bertholimule, Bertholimule, Bertholimule, Bertholimule. This Primary thought I was Purple, the Oranges were right behind me. I look to the hole in his shirt on his chest, Bertholimule. . .I just needed to stay calm, Purples were subservient, after he says his peace, I can get him to tell me where Bertholimule is.

" Yes, my Red?" I'll use as few words as possible, Red probably wasn't as close to this Purple as Blue was. I have a good shot of fooling him if the Oranges don't burst through the door and exclaim 'She's a fraud!' before dramatically tackling me to the ground.

" Did you sleep with my niece?" he asked seriously. . . .Are you

KIDDING ME?! Why on earth did this family have to be SO INVOLVED with their frickin' servants?! How was I, someone masquerading as Purple, SUPPOSED to know that answer?! If Purple was sleeping with the girl and Red already knew that, he was testing me. If I denied and it was true, he'd become angered, but if I denied it and he wasn't certain, then it'd be much better. Although he might respect my honesty, his body language screamed aggression, if I said I did. . .who knows what he'll do to me?! Who was his niece anyway?! Primaries didn't have siblings! Oh, this just wasn't fair. . .

" What?" I'd play dumb, " No, of course not, my Red." I made an expression of confused distressed. Red stood up and laced his fingers together, before pushing his arms out, stretching them. He was tall, his arms were thick, his shoulders were broad. His intimidation was working. " You're absolutely sure, Purple?" His sharp eyes flashed from his hands to me, his expression hard. " A little Primary girl, distressed and alone? You sure you could resist the temptation?" I frowned at him, playing a wholesome servant boy. " I promise you, my Red. I would never take advantage of my Blue like that. She's been very good to me." He paced closer and crossed his arms over his chest, " Has she? I bet she was pretty desperate after her father's death, well rest his soul. Are you sure nothing happened between you two?"

" Yes." I nodded, lowering my shoulders, " Please believe me, my Red." Red stared harshly and then gave a sigh. " Ok." He gave in with a shake of his head, " Just. . .don't hurt her." His eyes turned soft and tender, " She's in a vulnerable place right now. I think how you treat her will really affect her healing in this process. Don't you dare be selfish." He took a step forward and his eyes sharpened with anger. He brought his arms, tensed, to his sides. " You hurt her, you hurt one hair on her head, you bruise one feeble heart string-" He raised his pointer finger to me. " - Bertholimule isn't the only one who's going to end up dead." he finished with certainness.

" . . .What?" I couldn't help it, " Bertholimule?" Red pulled back some, his face becoming annoyed yet wondering.

" What of him?" My heart began to race faster and it was already in competition with a speeding train. " Where is he?" I asked, I tried but failed to keep the worry from my voice. Red cocked an eyebrow and stated, " In the dining room, right where he was earlier." He gave a wide grin, " Like right through those doors?" He lazily pointed a thumb to the doors he had been sitting in front of. " You forget?" he asked with a chuckle and a gaze that read, 'Colors, Purples are so dumb'. I walked quickly over to the

door, stepping around his watch chair and he didn't stop me. I
opened the doors.

Red

Purple disappeared inside the room and I rolled my eyes, heaven
only knew what that idiot wanted with Bertholimule.
Bertholimule. . . I brought one of my large hands to my chest
and rubbed over the torn part of my shirt, the skin feeling
smooth underneath. The kid had guts, I'd give him that, ripped
my fucking depon out of me. . . I don't think I'd ever been a
victim of something so violent, and from somebody who looked
like Blue. . . The hairs on my neck stood up. It was. . .I pressed
my hand tightly to the hole in my coat, not pleasant. Blue had
never done something to hurt me, he was the most gentle color I
knew. After the first time I had taken him, I worried how he'd
respond. He got up, silently left, and retreated back to his own
home. I had fretted the day he was to return. Perhaps he wouldn't
come, perhaps he had told Yellow and they both wouldn't come,
perhaps I'd spend the rest of my life alone, of course that was
before I'd had my kid. But then as I watched the skytrain from
my window, he stepped out, holding Blue's hand with a smile.
Blue just a toddling, stuttering thing then, always smiling and,
just as quickly, throwing pouting fits. Her moods changed like
ocean tides, rose and fell, and he adored her, he always had,
always would. His eyes just sparkled when he looked at her, as if

the world's finest jewel was before his eyes. And I, as I watched from my tall, far away window, wanted those eyes for myself. I would hold my hand over my heart and feel as if it was glowing, swelling, I was beyond mesmerized by him. I was hopelessly in love with him.

. . .We spoke at dinner as if nothing had happened and if I closed my eyes and pretended, nothing had. Yellow and him would chastise me about when I was going to bear as usual and I chuckled as much as I cursed them. We were all so young then, Yellow's son was two years older than Blue, and as the oldest child, he still regularly wet his bed. We all wet our beds at one point, well Primaries did anyway, it was nice to know we all came from the same helpless beginning. As they'd chatter and we'd eat, I'd stare at Blue and he had to-had to know how I felt about him. I felt I couldn't hide it if I tried! In my mind, it permeated through my skin and made this choking fog around me, trapping me in, making me blind. I didn't blame either of us; it was just the way it was. Primaries didn't court each other, we didn't have relationships, but everyone had touched themselves, everyone knew of the Secondaries' affairs. Why couldn't I have him? I would have him.

Unfortunately, he wasn't as enthusiastic as I was and I thought he'd get used to it, he'd learn to enjoy it, he'd want to be with me, it was only a matter of time, right? But he. . .didn't. He always left before dark, he always tried to push me away, he always begged me to stop, and so I grew bitter. He hated me. . . How could he HATE ME?! Didn't he know how much I loved him?! Why? Did he not care? He was so-so selfish!

I hoped once I gave in to their constant harassment and bore a stupid child, maybe the anger and void in my life would disappear. . .but it never did. My child was just a bother, a chore, a duty I was obliged to perform. I let my Purple do most of the rearing. I didn't really want it. But I wanted Blue, wanted him like a poisoned color wants an antidote; desperately. And yet I could never have him. . .not his body, but his heart, it wasn't MINE! He teased me like that, so kind to me, so kind to my child, but so fucking merciless, so fucking sadistic, dangling the medicine to save my life centimeters from my hands. . .

Bertholimule couldn't fill the space that Blue left inside me. For even when I was inside Blue, he was never inside me. His love never was, it never reached me and I was left crushingly empty. .
.

" My Red!" I was torn back to reality. " What?" I spat irritably and saw Orange and Yellow's Orange charging down the hall. " Purple!" My Orange skidded to a halt in front of me, " We can't find him!"

" Why would you-"

" Please, my Red!" Yellow's Orange insisted, his voice warm caramel. I turned my head to the dining room's closed doors. I walked towards them slowly and the Oranges watched and then, I heard their boot-clad feet hurry to get on either side of me. I opened the doors and before my table, stood Bertholimule in his loose black shirt and pants, tall, moccasin-like boots, armed with a fierce, bloated face.

Purple stood next to him in a combat stance. Bertholimule used a red cloth napkin from the table, already in hand, to wipe his face and then dropped the blue coated fabric to the floor. He stood tall and brought his chest out. I grinned but. . .my spirit wasn't in it. My spirit was out roaming the mansion grounds trying to find Blue in every wind breeze, and every leaf's crunch.

Blue

Purple, in Turquoise's body, and I walked down the hall. I had grown impatient. " Maybe we should wait?" he asked quietly, " Turquoise could be dangerous."

" Oh, she's dangerous." I replied and he asked, " Uh, how do you-"

" I saw her kill a color."

" What?!" I turned my head back to him, " Bertholimule and Turquoise had a peasant team of three. How many filthy terrorists are in our house?" Purple made an awkward expression, looking pretty yet worn as Turquoise. The peasant had thick lashes and a long nose with a sharp, angled end. She had thick brows and flat-broad lips, her face had the look of someone who believed they had seen too much of life but had barely seen enough, I'd gather she was about my. . .father's age.

" Two?" Purple answered unsurely. I nodded, " What do you think they did with the other three?" Purple frowned and looked down to the floor, " I guess they. . .got rid of them?" He glanced back to me with wariness to conform with suspicion. Well at least he had some sense in that tiny brain of his.

With a nod, I thought of how Bertholimule had confessed it to me not less than forty minutes ago. 'Disposed of' he had said, I shuddered with disgust, 'I had no need for them anymore.' What kind of remorseless man said things like that? Turquoise had killed one of their teammates too, they were nothing more than murderers to me. Those peasants got what they deserved for being involved in my father's death but now it was time their judges receive some retribution. Yellow may want more answers but I had all the answers I needed. He was a cold-souled killer, and his hours were limited. Those were my answers. Justice would only happen when we strung Bertholimule up to where my father had fallen down from. What goes down, must go up. For I would pull it there, pull it there kicking and screaming.

" And you. . .saw that?" Purple asked, eyes wide and aghast. " Yes." I replied and sighed, " And I wouldn't wish anyone see it again." I began to pace down the hall, I had ended up stopping. " I'm beginning to think nothing good comes from death, Purple." He trailed behind me and my vision of the red corridor bobbed slightly with my paces, as your sight often does when walking, wandering, running. Only when you stood still did your eyes not change the world around you. How powerful yet. . .frightening.

" But I. . .thought you wanted to kill Bertholimule?" Purple stated and I didn't even stop to glare over my shoulder.

" Death and justice are not the same thing." I answered with strong, calm confidence. " Except for today, today they are. . ." I smiled and fisted a hand in front of me. Today they are. . .

Bertholimule

My ropes lay on the ground, Turquoise stood beside me. A lot had happened to me today, I confessed not all, ok most things, hadn't gone according to plan but, so was life. And my life wasn't over yet. These Primaries had execution in mind for me and even if it wasn't quite that, I didn't think I favored a life trapped away in a dingy cell. I faced Red who was grinning like he enjoyed this display more than a theatre play. His eyes went from Turquoise to me, the Oranges on either side of him had their hands on their swords. I wish I had a weapon, if Red were taller than me, the Oranges were grand oak trees and me an acorn. Still I didn't let my nervous anticipation show, I kept a straight, hard face.

" Count me impressed." Red stated, placing his hands on his hips, " You managed to get one of our own Secondaries to betray us. Years of loyalty and conditioning gone; poof," He made a gesture with his hand; a fast expanding of fingers, " Just like that, Bertholimule. You know. . ." His eyes narrowed, " I'm starting to doubt your story. A Blue? Raised with no witnesses except dead peasants, never any sign of him, for years?" He cocked a hip to the side and asked, " You're Blue, aren't you? Why would Purple be loyal to a stranger, it's you, isn't it?" His eyes gazed at me and once again I could have lied, but they would have figured me out eventually. Maybe not Red cause he seemed desperate to believe his friend was alive, but the others would know and at some point, they would have to acknowledge that. No charade lasts forever. " What will it take to get you to believe me?" I asked, irritated.

" Proof!" he retorted, taking a step forward. " Then let's go get his body!" I announced and Red's eyes grew wide. " Let's go get it!" I repeated, " You can take your Oranges, and I can show you, that I'm not him."

Red quieted and his face relaxed, his eyes growing wide, they glossed over. He said, " Then go. . ." I blinked widely in shock, he looked away and tears dropped down startlingly red from his eyes. The Oranges looked to him in surprise, " If you truly have taken the only man I ever loved away, then go." I looked to Turquoise in Purple's body, wondering what to do. She nodded to me. I looked back and I began to slowly approach the door.

Red stepped back, turning around, and the Oranges hesitated a moment longer and then followed him. " My Red," one said sheepishly, " Blue wanted us to capture Purple."

" Purple?" Red replied, and as I crossed through the doorway, he drug an arm across his face. " Wait." He turned back to me, " Yes?" I said with a calmness hiding inner uncertainty. " How did you charm our Purple? They're not an easy replacement, leave him."

" I have left him." I returned, now standing in the foyer. " This is my teammate Turquoise in Purple's body. He's in hers." Red blinked widely and I imagined the Oranges were utterly confused although it was somewhat hard to determine their emotions through their visors. " How did you manage that?" Red asked and I answered, " Through that technique I used on you." He looked startled, " You used that on a peasant?" He visually recoiled and looked disgusted, he smiled weakly, " You really aren't Blue. You have no respect for tradition." I shrugged and stated, " Come on, Turquoise, we're going." She was already right behind me, she nodded and we walked to the front doors.

I didn't know where I was going but I couldn't stay here. It was too dangerous but- I placed a hand on the knob-. . .where else was there to go? My face still stung and my arm still had a cramp but, what was there for me outside these walls? I could return to my parents' home and tell the trees all about my adventure or. . .I could remain here and see what awaited me. I bet they wouldn't kill me, I was a Primary and more important, they were a bunch of soft-hearted family men and women. Even Red, who seemed the most fearless among them, had cried over his friend. If they were going to kill me, wouldn't they have done it by now? Maybe I was just wishing it so but. . .I was out of options. I couldn't exactly go live among the common people without causing society to breakdown. I had no choice. I had come to be Blue and hell, I wasn't him but I was A BLUE and I wouldn't be shoved aside so easily. I wouldn't be disposed of, be dismissed, and only remembered as a queer story. I didn't know anything about myself and the cabin didn't have any answers, only here did and so here is where I would remain. I turned around and Turquoise startled.

" Bertholimule?" she asked quietly, " I can't leave." I whispered in return. She frowned in her foreign features. She shook her head no. " They'll kill you. . ." I smiled slightly, " They can try." She pleaded, " We could be happy together back on the mountaintop, Bertholimule." I glanced to Red, who stood staring sharply at me. I glanced back to her, " Until you die." I reminded, staring her straight in the eyes. I tenderly hoped she'd understand, her now purple eyes seemed lost in grief. I held under her chin softly and pulled her lips to mine. She laced her hands around my neck and I grabbed her tightly around the waist. Her, Purple's, lips were dry, he needed some water. I pulled away and whispered, " Trust me." She closed her eyes and assured, " Always."

" Ummmm," I looked over to Red, who looked irritated. " Hello? Leaving?" The two Oranges looked stiff as twigs. I released Turquoise and turned to him, " Red, I think we should have a talk." He gave a growl, " I'm done talking! I gave you a direct order, peasant boy!"

" I do not want to leave." I stated firmly, he blinked widely in confusion. " Are you kidding me? If you stay-"

" Blue will try to kill me, I know." I took on my best revolutionist voice, the one I would play with for my subjects. " But Yellow doesn't seem set on that plan," I took a step forward, " And neither do you."

" Me?!" he exclaimed with protest, pressing a hand to his chest, " I don't care if you live or die! I really don't!" He crossed his arms over this chest. With a frown, I stated, " No, you want me alive." I took another step forward. " Because I look like your lover." Red was splashed with surprise, he shook his head no. " O-of course, I don't-"

" You already took a side in encouraging me to leave. Just admit that you want me, Red." He looked flustered now.

" What the f-" I was in front of him now, " If you vouch for me, that's two against one. Blue is just a girl, what can she do on her own?" He looked distressed, the Oranges had a hand on their blade handles. I needed to be careful. " Together I can stay." I ran a hand through his hair and sweat dripped down his face. One of the Oranges stepped forward and pushed me away. " That's enough." Her voice was high, female, she looked back to Red, who was staring at me in a state of processing. " My Red, we're here to protect you, and I don't know exactly what's going on, but I know my duty and am committed to that." She glanced to me to make sure I hadn't moved and then looked back to Red. " Is there anything you want me to do?" Red stared past her to me. He blinked and said, " I really do recommend you leave, nothing good has ever been done to a Blue within these walls. . ."

I couldn't read his expression. I nodded and trusted myself to fate or random chance, " I am certain."

" Orange, Oranges." Red stated, placing a hand on Orange's shoulder, his eyes didn't leave mine. " Make sure these two don't go anywhere." He turned and wandered off to the stairs, a hand to his mouth.

Blue

" What are 'you' doing untied from your chair?!" I stormed into the foyer and Purple hurried his feet to stay behind me. The Oranges startled and I turned my head to them with anger. " I told you to capture Purple! What are you two DOING with these unrestrained prisoners?!"

" My Blue, please." the Female Orange began, only identifiable by her voice, the Oranges looked nearly identical in their armor and helmets. " Red asked us to keep them here."

" Greetings, Blue." Bertholimule said. I hated the sound of his voice, it was so freakin' versatile. He sounded like a school boy tenor right now but I knew he could drop it like a rock to the darkest parts of the bass range. My father's voice never unnaturally jumped around like that.

" I'm not talking to you, trash can!" He smiled and rolled his eyes. His unfrightened arrogance made me hate him more than I already did! Which was a ton! " Where are Yellow and Red?" I demanded to the Oranges. Why would they leave this murderer unattended?! And more importantly why wasn't he trying to run? The door was right there, I hadn't exactly made my intentions for him secretive.

Bertholimule brought his hand out as he informed, " Yellow is checking the official records and Red went to find her." My eye twitched, " Once again, trash bag, I didn't ask you!" Purple tapped my shoulder and I looked at him with irritation. " Turquoise." he said, looking guilty for interrupting me. I looked back to my servant's body across the floor. Turquoise stared at me harshly from inside it.

" Switch back already." I stated and Turquoise looked to me with seriousness and then glanced to Bertholimule.

Bertholimule grinned to me, " YOU were the one who figured it out?" he asked with disbelief. I nodded stonily. " I know my Purple better than I know my own mind."

Bertholimule shrugged, " But isn't he below you? Shouldn't a Primary be more detached from their Secondaries?" I scoffed, "

You don't know anything about us, so stop pretending like you do. You're nothing but a killer." A disgusting smirk grew from his peeled blue lips.

" Perhaps, but at least that is something. What are you, Blue? Who are you? An orphan?" He chuckled and looked back to Turquoise. I frowned, that hitting me firmly in the chest. An orphan. . .I guess I was. . .

" Switch back." I said to Turquoise again, although it sounded less determined than before. She looked to Bertholimule and with a brush of his hair, a careless grin on his face, he said, " Go ahead, the jig is already up."

" Alright." Purple's voice said, she straightened up and took a step forward, " But he's getting the short end of the deal." It seemed nothing changed and we stood in silence. Then Purple stated, " I'm back, . . .my Blue." He sounded miserable as always. Turquoise walked past me, fluffing her surprisingly well kept hair out, and Purple trudged gingerly past Bertholimule. They crossed each other on the floor and Turquoise leaned up on her toes and whispered something into Bertholimule's ear once she arrived beside him. He nodded, smiling, and closed his eyes in peace. Purple came and when I looked at him, he awkwardly looked away; he went to stand behind me. I huffed out some frustrated air and wished he'd be at least a little more happy to be back in his own body! I mean that was a pretty big deal! He was so lifeless! Like a dead fish pulled from the sea, sad glossy eyes, wretched at everything! Static in its despondency. I don't think I'd ever seen him happy. . .

" By the way, Purple," Bertholimule addressed directly, " you really should get a glass of water, your lips are dry as desert sand." I looked to my servant and he cocked a brow, " Um. . .how do you know that?" Purple asked in return.

" Oh yeah and you should get that injury on your leg attended to." Turquoise added and I blinked widely in surprise, she looked to me and stated, " He's got a bum leg right now."

" Purple!" I snapped, " Why didn't you tell me?!" He looked victimized, " But you haven't gotten your wounds attended to either, my Blue! Why does it matter?"

" Of course it doesn't matter THAT much but you should have at least told me about it!" He gave a look of surprise, then anger. He looked away, " Maybe you don't matter THAT much. . ." he mumbled under his breath. I grit my teeth but felt a stream of sadness open up in my chest, of sadness like soaking blood. I. . .I didn't mean it like that, I meant like. . .I didn't mean to say he didn't matter.

" Wow, Blue." Bertholimule jeered, " I wish I was your servant, that seems like a delightful experience."

" Shut it, trash can!" My tone wasn't filled with the same amount of venom it had had at the beginning of this conversation, it had lessened significantly. Now I just wanted him to be quiet, although I'm not sure why, it never hurt as bad in the noise.

" Listen, Blue," my father's killer retorted, " you're going to have to get used to me being around, I'm not going anywhere."

" You're going six feet under." I assured darkly. He smirked, " So you think but the only one going that far underneath is your father." My eyes widened and they glossed over with tears. Every claim I made about how evil Bertholimule was, they were all true. I looked down to the floor and was filled with so much stirring anger and grief. An ocean of it.

" Why-I-" I bit my lip, no. I had nothing to say. Like everyone else, I'd walk away. I turned and wordlessly retreated to the stairs to fall apart by myself, just as I'm sure Yellow and Red were doing. I'm sure the record scrolls were codeword for drinks full of teardrops. Couldn't count on those two for anything.

Blue

I had wandered up the stairs, one flight, another, anything to keep moving forward when the past weighed you down and drug you back. I wished the stairs were endless, I wish there was a true escape, but there wasn't. . .you just had to keep walking, even if it was slowly, even if it was one step at a time. Walk, walk slowly, or shrivel up and die. Eventually I was on floor four or five, a little out of breath and legs feeling like jelly. I heaved over and some tears wet my eyes. I was breathing heavy. In and out. In and out. Dad was dead. In and out. Out and in. His killer was currently in the foyer. In and out. Purple didn't love me. Out and in. He probably never had. In, out, in, out, thus was all of our fates. . .as harsh as this, as brutal, as heartbreaking, that is life. In and out, of relationships, of trouble, of peace. A tumultuous, dynamic sea of everyday change.

I righted and began to walk. I moved like in a trance, slowly, thoughtlessly, running a hand along the wall. Oceans rolled and changed and were bombarded with constant storms. They had to deal with beautiful coral and deadly sharks, but through it all they touched the sky; they remained.

A door opened a ways in front of me. Red's Purple stepped out and she spotted me with a bright smile, she hurried over to me, pulling an angry looking Young Red with her.

" My Blue," she said as she began to travel towards me. She looked so real then, something I couldn't ignore, the way her neck muscles strained her skin, the endless down to up slide of her shoulders as she walked, her skin smooth, flesh purple. " How are you, my Blue? I'm so sorry to bother you. Where is Purple? If you don't mind saying."

" He's downstairs, I left him in the foyer." My voice didn't even sound like my own but then, did I even know what my voice sounded like? Had I ever paused and wondered what others heard? Had I ever screamed as loud as I could, till my throat was completely dry? Had I ever just looked into my mirror and spoke to myself? Told myself about everything I saw, everything I felt? Had I ever really told myself I loved her?

Had I ever licked her skin? Did I know the taste of the flesh I walked around in? What were you? Body? Soul? Essence? . . .Blue?

" D-do you think, I'm so sorry to ask this but-"

" You can go see him." She smiled widely and bowed, " Thank you, thank you, my Blue! How kind and noble of you!"

" It's not fair, you're so mean, my Blue! I never asked for this place! I never wanted it!"

" Blue. You're desperate and it's honestly trying, try and tone it down."

" Not everything is about you, Blue. You're such a bitch."

" What are you, Blue? Who are you? An orphan?"

I didn't know what I was, I didn't know who I was. " The Ocean." A tear dropped down my face and I thought, I'm not sure you're right, Father.

" Oh, my Blue!" Purple exclaimed in worry, " Are you ok?" She reached her hands out in concern and I hit one of them away. " I'm fine!" I wiped at my weak eye and turned so only my side was facing her. " I'll watch Red for a bit, go see him." Purple, with wide eyes, looked between me and the child and for a moment, hesitated. Then she said, " Yes, of course." She bowed again, " Thank you, my Blue."

" Don't leave me with Blue!" Red protested in his high annoying voice, " She doesn't listen!" Purple sighed, and assured with a weak smile, " I'll be back, sweetie." and kissed the top of his head. " Ew!" he protested and pushed her away. Then she gave me an equally guilty and grateful glance and ran off down the hall. Red glared daggers at her running frame. " What a stupidhead." he said, with pouting cheeks and a clenched glare. Then he looked to me and I stared to him with deadness. " Why were you crying, Blue?" he asked ignorantly.

" Because my dad's dead." I answered. He cocked a brow and looked at me skeptically, " Dumb Blue, Primaries don't die." I frowned and was filled with an exploding firework of anguish. " But they do!" What was I even doing?! He was eight.

" No-no!" he fought, " Daddy says Primaries don't. We're Primaries!"

" Well, he's a liar! We do!" Red glared at me and swore, " I ain't ever gonna die!" I frowned and walked a step to the wall, I sunk down and placed my chin on my pulled up knees. Red blinked widely at me, he was in his red nightgown with lace and buttons, the whole sha-bang. We stood and sat in silence for not more than a minute before Red said, in his squeaky, little voice, " I'm still going to marry you."

" Nothing like a good passionate fuck before a bath, right Blue?" I physically flinched and looked around. A hand balancing myself on the red carpet of the hall, I thought, what on Earth. . .

" Are you listening, Blue?" I looked to him in surprise. That had been his father's voice but, but that didn't make any sense. Red wasn't here and-and I had never heard him say that? So-so why did that appear in my mind? " Blue, you better listen to me." I looked up and saw those narrowed, unhappy eyes.

" Red, I'm. . .listening."

" Good!" the child announced, " Cause I don't want to talk to a color without them listening." I nodded and put a hand on my chest, my pleated, wrinkled dress smooth under my soft palm. He sat down criss-cross applesauce and said, " What kind of dress do you want to wear at our wedding?" I stared at him dryly with squinted eyes. " What is this marriage nonsense you're always spewing?" I asked, irritably, I had the odd feeling that was something peasants did.

" It's when you love someone and you live with them." Red explained simply, " I don't wanna be lonely, so I'm going to marry you. Daddy is always busy, so if I get married to you then I won't be alone anymore." I frowned and such a notion made me uncomfortable. " What if I don't want to get married?" Red frowned, " Why wouldn't you want to?" he asked, putting one of his cheeks in his hand.

I frowned, " Because that's not something a Primary does. We do not 'marry'." He scowled and shook his head, " They do! Dumb Blue, dumb!"

I gritted my teeth, " Well, I don't."

" You will!" he claimed and I slammed my head into my knees, knowing how pointless and stupid this argument was! We sat in more silence, he started talking again, I decided not to listen. I closed my eyes and I had this image of a beach, rocks jutting from the water, white-white sand so soft and sticky, this endless sky, soaring birds, and then the Ocean. It sparkled with the sun's light and I felt my smile widening. I had no idea where the image came from, for it was nothing like the beach father had often taken me to.

" Blue! Blue! BLUE!" Red was tapping on my shoulder, " What?!" I snapped, looking up. His eyes grew wide and then he looked angry, " You weren't listening again!"

" Please Red, " I pleaded, I was so done right now, " I can't do this right now. Please stop." He held my gaze, my eyes sad and miserable, his fierce and burning. " . . .Wanna play trucks?" he asked after a moment. " Trucks?" I questioned. He nodded and jumped up.

" Come on!" He ran to the open door and slowly, my body feeling older than it did a few minutes ago, I rose too, following him.

He showed me his collection of toy trucks, he had a lot of them. Little trucks, big trucks, monster trucks. " You're the blue truck." he explained and handed me a blue model pick-up truck. " Ok." I said, lacking energy. " I'm the fire truck." he explained with importance. I sat down on my knees and he plopped down on his butt. He paused, holding the metal and plastic toy in his hand. "

Blue?"

" Yes, Red?" He looked like he was thinking really hard. He rolled his truck slowly on the ground, " If your dad's dead, will I not get to see him anymore?" I frowned, the child looked to me with suddenly very sad eyes. I sighed out sadly, " I'm afraid so." I said quietly. His brow furrowed and he brought a hand to his chin, " I don't really understand." he confessed shamelessly. I shrugged, " Me neither . . . I just. . ." He looked to me, " It feels like he'll come walking right through that door," I pointed wistfully out his bedroom door and smiled weakly. The smile faded, leaving my devastated expression in its place.

" Well I trust my daddy." Red reminded, " Maybe he'll come back." I shook my head and looked down to my blue pick-up, " I don't think so, Red." The wind whistled against the closed window. I looked out. It was day now, maybe noon. This time yesterday father and I were traveling over the countryside in the skytrain. He was staring to the earth and I was listening to what he had to say. That hurt me so much. These twenty-four hours have hurt me so much.

" Wait?" Red asked, as if he had just remembered something. " Who's my daddy gonna marry? He wanted to marry your dad." I smiled, what a sweet childish concern. A laugh left me, I shrugged, " Maybe he can marry Bertholimule!" The image of Bertholimule in a wedding dress and Red in a groom's suit was so funny to me. Although, I thought I didn't know anything about weddings. I laughed and laughed and Little Red began to laugh with me. Then he asked, " Who's Bertholimule?" through the laughter. I continued to laugh and my soul felt slightly less burdened. Things would be ok. I had hope here. I had Blue here. I could live on. Everyone within this mansion can live on and you can too, no matter what you're going through. You can live here too. Color yourself Blue.

Acknowledgments

I wanted to give a big thank you to my family for helping me in every way they can. Mom, you're amazing and your support for me, and my writing, always brings a bright warmth into my heart. I wanted to thank you for helping me to edit this book too, you didn't have to do that and you caught a lot of typos I miraculously overlooked. So thank you, I love you. David, bro, thanks for always reading my work and putting up with my moods. Your time and patience means a lot to me. I treasure our long talks about character, plot, Undertale fanfiction, and everything in between. Toby, you're my favorite. Gabi, you're an adorable, feisty sunflower who will take this world by storm, don't ever forget that. Dad, thanks for always being the rock I and our family needs you to be. I hope the homosexual content in this book didn't traumatize you too much. I also wanted to thank God, for giving me such an amazing family and also granting me my passion, and drive, to write and create. Without His guidance and patience, I wouldn't be the still changing man I am now. I also wanted to thank modern medicine for allowing me to not slowly agonizingly die, that's always a bonus. I wanted to also thank anyone and everyone who bought and read a copy of my first novel *Stars*. It was and is really special to me. Anyone who took their valuable time, and hard earned money, to support a young and eager artist like me, is truly a special kind of wonderful. As for everything else, I pretty much did it all myself. Peace out, don't give up on your dreams, yada yada, rock on, you shiny diamond.

About The Author/Tell Me What You Think

Daniel Stone is a crazy, weirdo boy who lives in Maryland and drinks copious amounts of black tea and likes to obsess over fictional characters. He's a starving artist and has barely got his life together. He also LOVES input. So give him some! Love this book? Hate it? Somewhere in the middle? Tell him about it! Leave a review on Amazon.com, after searching up Color Me Blue by Daniel Stone, or visit his Goodreads page at https://www.goodreads.com/author/show/17879228.Daniel_Stone and leave a review. His contact email for any business ventures is at danielschlueteroffical@gmail.com . Feel free to check out his first novel *Stars* if you liked this one, or even if you didn't, for they're very different in tone. God bless! Remember to smile!

Made in the USA
Middletown, DE
22 May 2019